Title Run

The Run

Title Run

Anthony Hampshire

Fitzhenry & Whiteside

Published in Canada by Fitzhenry & Whiteside,
195 Allstate Parkway, Markham, Ontario L3R 4T8

Published in the United States by Fitzhenry & Whiteside,
311 Washington Street, Brighton, Massachusetts 02135

www.fitzhenry.ca   godwit@fitzhenry.ca

10 9 8 7 6 5 4 3 2 1

Fitzhenry & Whiteside acknowledges with thanks the Canada Council
for the Arts and the Ontario Arts Council for their support of our
publishing program. We acknowledge the financial support of
the Government of Canada through the Book Publishing Industry
Development Program (BPIDP) for our publishing activities.

Library and Archives Canada Cataloguing in Publication
Hampshire, Anthony, 1951-
Title run / Anthony Hampshire.
(Redline racing series)
ISBN 1-55041-566-2
I. Title. II. Series.
PS8565.A5663T57 200   jC813'.6   C2005-905226-0

**U.S. Publisher Cataloging-in-Publication Data
(Library of Congress Standards)**

Hampshire, Anthony, 1951-
Title run / Anthony Hampshire.
[138] p. : cm. (Redline racing series)
Summary: Racing driver Eddie and his team have vaulted up
the standing of the North America Formula Atlantic series,
and one more win will give them the title; but Eddie is offered
a long-term racing deal, which comes with a sacrifice
that could break up his team for good.
ISBN 1-55041-566-2 (pbk.)
1. Automobile racing — Juvenile literature — Fiction. I. Title.
II. Series. [Fic] —dc22   PZ7.H34Ti 2005

Design by Wycliffe Smith Design Inc.
Cover photo courtesy of Eric Gilbert, Motorsport.com

Printed in Canada

For Maureen, Ali, and Cait.
You were right!
—*A.H.*

ACKNOWLEDGEMENTS

I am very grateful to my editor Ann Featherstone, whose insight and thoroughness have greatly improved this story; and to Gail Winskill at Fitzhenry & Whiteside for her constant support and encouragement. I owe a special debt of gratitude to Justin Sofio, driver for the Mathiasen Motorsports/RLM Investments Formula Atlantic team in California, and to Cam Binder of Binder Racing in Calgary. Justin and Cam graciously adopted me as a crew member, patiently answered all of my technical questions about their Swift 008 race car, and even gave me an official team hat.

Chapter 1

Clarence and Alfie

Y ou like surprises, don't you, Eddie?" Caroline asked.

"That depends," I replied carefully. It did depend. Birthday and Christmas surprises were fun because someone had planned them to be that way. Then there were the other kind—the unplanned ones, which were usually accidents and turned out to be fun for everyone, except me. Like the time last winter when the crew chief of our race team, Herb MacDonald, asked me to pull the oil pan off the tow truck's engine. Unfortunately, he forgot to tell me that it was still full of oil. I found *that* out lying on my back under the truck as I carefully removed the last bolt, wiggled the pan loose…and, surprise! Six quarts of thick black sludge poured onto my hair. Took me a week of shampoos with paint thinner to get it all out.

Then there was the time this spring when I took the battery out of my dad's boat in Vancouver and lugged it into the marina to get a new one. As I carried it down the long pier, some of the battery acid must have leaked out the vent caps and onto my waist. I finally put it down and reached into my pocket for some money…and, surprise! The front of my coveralls fell off.

So, yes, I know something about surprises. As it wasn't my birthday and as Christmas was five months away, I was being careful. Plus, at that point all I really wanted to do was sleep.

I was finishing my fourth grinding day behind the wheel of our black Dodge truck, pulling a thirty-five-foot box trailer with our Swift race car inside. We were on the last leg of a trek all the way from Toronto, Ontario, to Miami, Florida, for the final race in the North American Formula Atlantic Series. After covering six states and over 2,000 miles of blistering hot pavement, we were only half an hour from our destination in West Palm Beach. I was in no mood for surprises. I was, however, absolutely in the mood for a long, hot shower and about sixteen hours of sleep.

Caroline Grant, our team manager, sat next to me in the front seat of the Dodge. Herb snored contentedly in the back, as he had done since leaving Toronto after our first race win five days ago. The rest of the team followed behind us in my Aunt Sophie's enormous motor home. We were on our way to the vacation home of John and Susan Reynolds, the owners of DynaSport Industries and the sponsors of our team. The plan was to relax for a few days before the final race on the oval in Homestead, Florida, and they had arrived from New York that morning and set up quarters for everyone. Sun, sand, and relaxation—and no surprises. Or so I thought.

I found the right road and was expecting to pull up in front of some tired little beach house with faded, peeling yellow paint, a few palm trees, and maybe a creaky rowboat—your basic cottage or vacation home. Instead, we followed a long stone driveway and stepped out of our vehicles to find a huge, two-story mansion of rock and glass that had its own private beach, a wharf, and three powerboats. It could have passed for a small hotel. After almost a week on the road, it looked like the perfect place to relax for a long weekend until race week started.

With eight bedrooms, all with an ocean view, I expected that each of us would have our own rooms, and everyone did...except me. Susan informed me that I had the largest guest room, but there was a catch. I had to share it with Clarence and Alfie. Both she and Caroline seemed to know all about this arrangement and couldn't wait for me to meet them. I remembered Caroline's question and had a feeling that this was the setup for my big surprise. Everyone else ran to check out the beach while Caroline, Susan, and I carried bags and assorted gear into the house and climbed the open staircase up to the second-floor corner bedroom.

"So, are Clarence and Alfie your kids, Susan?" I asked.

She considered my question carefully for a moment.

"Our kids? Oh yes. I'd say so."

"I didn't know you guys had kids."

Susan smiled. "Well, they're not in school or anything, Eddie. They're um…they're too young."

"How old are they?"

"Two and three. J.R. calls them 'the Lads.' They're both bundles of energy and very cute. I know that they'll just love you…Uncle Eddie," she beamed.

Uncle Eddie? Little kids are fun and everything, but sharing a room with two preschool boys with strange names for the next three days was definitely not my idea of relaxation. I knew what it would be like. There would be piggyback rides on Uncle Eddie, art projects, reading the same stories over and over again, cookie crumbs, and conversations in four-word sentences. It would be loud, messy, and sticky—seventy-two hours of nonstop babysitting. It would not be relaxing. It might even be scary.

We reached the top of the stairs and started down the hallway toward the double oak-paneled doors of the largest bedroom. I stopped and put down my bags. I needed a way out—and fast.

"Susan, look. I just don't feel right just barging in and taking Lawrence and Alfie's—"

"*Clarence*, Eddie," she replied firmly. "He won't answer to Lawrence."

"Sorry.... Clarence. Anyway, I can't just take over their bedroom. What if I just sleep in the motor home?"

She thought this over, then shook her head. "No. You'd break their little hearts. They'd cry all night, poor things. They're dying to meet you, Eddie. I told them all about you and Caroline on the way down from New York."

There it was—my way out. Caroline, *Auntie* Caroline, loved little kids, and she had the warmth, patience, and creativity to deal with them. She was a natural.

"Well, Susan, don't you think they'd be far more

comfortable bunking with Auntie Caroline? And don't worry; I'll help her look after them. We'll play beach football...do shark attacks in the water...have ice cream fights...and build sandcastles and blow them up. All that guy stuff."

Susan and Caroline exchanged a quick glance, then they both turned away from me, stifling their laughter and struggling for control. Something was going on that I knew nothing about. I was rapidly coming to the conclusion that there was a plot here.

Susan regained her composure and faced me. "Guy stuff, you think, Eddie? Sounds like fun. They do love the water."

Caroline crossed to the bedroom doors, opened one a crack, and whispered, "Eddie, come here, quietly—shhh. They're sleeping. Just peek in. Clarence's bed is the first one. Alfie's is by the window. They're so cute."

I padded over to the door and stuck my head in slowly.

Clarence was sprawled across the nearest bed. His head drooped off the end. His tongue hung out of the side of his mouth and his feet were in the air. Alfie was curled into a ball inside a mound of blankets and rubber toys, with only his nose sticking out.

"Didn't I tell you they were adorable?" Susan whispered as she joined us.

I got it. Clarence and Alfie, my surprise roommates, were not preschoolers. They were not the Reynolds' children.

They were dogs.

Chapter 2

A New Friend

The stillness was shattered as Caroline flung open the door, cried, "Puppies!" and dropped to her knees. The Lads awoke instantly, bolted from their beds, and scrambled across the carpet to welcome her.

Clarence was a large, black Labrador retriever with liquid brown eyes, a soft mouth, and a wagging tail that could move small pieces of furniture. Alfie was a rust-and-white Welsh corgi, built low to the ground on short, sturdy legs, with only a stump for a tail and a face like a fox. Both dogs were bullet fast, and they launched into Caroline, bowling her over and licking her face mercilessly.

"Eddie! Help!" she shrieked with delight.

I dropped to the floor and thumped the carpet to get their attention. Both of them stopped the welcoming assault on Caroline and looked at me for a second.

Clarence bounded over almost immediately, but Alfie stared curiously, cocked his head sideways, and then slowly crept over to sniff my socks. He was taking the time to check out the new guy.

I scratched Clarence behind his big, floppy ears and told him what a big, strong dog he was. He closed his eyes in delight, and I knew that I had made a friend for life. Alfie was more cautious, but as soon as he saw Clarence getting all the attention, he abandoned my socks, sat down in front of me, and firmly placed one of his white paws on my leg. I shook it. I stroked his ears flat and told him how handsome he was. He wiggled. When they were happy, Clarence lashed the air with his long, black tail and Alfie wiggled his entire body. It appeared that I'd passed the test.

"See?" Caroline announced. "They love you, Eddie. Don't you, you bad boys?"

Caroline stroked their silky heads and talked to them in that soft, cooing voice that girls reserve for smiling babies and loyal dogs.

"Great guard dogs, Susan. They'd lick a burglar to death," I observed dryly.

"No, they wouldn't. They bark very loudly when they're upset. But they're not upset now—are you, boys? No, because Uncle Eddie is here. Yes, Clarence! A new friend."

Something clicked in Clarence's small brain the moment he heard the word "friend." His eyes opened wide. He leapt up and then placed his jaws firmly around my left wrist. It wasn't painful like a bite—more like a warm, wet clamp. I tried to pull my arm free but Clarence was having none of it. I was caught and about to be retrieved.

Clarence led me by the wrist out of the bedroom, down the stairs, and out the front door. Then I was tugged back into the house, through the living room, into the kitchen, laundry room, TV room, downstairs bathroom, through the sliding doors to the outdoor deck, back inside, up the stairs, into the second-floor bathrooms, into all eight bedrooms, and back downstairs again to the front door. The tour took about two minutes, after which Clarence finally released my wrist and sat proudly looking up at Alfie, who had watched the spectacle with Caroline and Susan from the second-floor balcony.

The others returned from the beach, came in through the sliding deck doors, and saw us standing at the front entrance.

"Welcome, Eddie," John Reynolds laughed. "I see you've just had the royal tour. Clarence will do that for the first few days if you're new and he likes you. He just wants you to know you're welcome in his house, and he'll show you where everything is so you won't get lost.

Clarence isn't too bright; Alfie is the clever one but Clarence will always look after you."

Clarence looked up at me, barked once, and smiled in that goofy way that only Labs can. I'd been on the tour, and now we were pals. I looked at him and then pointed to Rick Grant—Caroline's brother, our race team designer, and one of my best friends. It was time to share.

"Clarence, look! A *friend!*"

Rick was immediately clamped and dragged off. As the afternoon went on, I used the magic word to make sure that everyone had the tour. After all, what fun is a surprise if you can't enjoy it with your friends?

Chapter 3

Recharging

W e spent the next four days as the Reynolds' guests, swimming, water skiing, snorkeling, sun tanning, and playing shark attack with Clarence and Alfie. Rick and Herb became restless by Monday of race week. They drove north to spend a few days in Orlando, where they had found an aircraft shop to build and test Rick's latest rear wing. Rick was confident it would be even better than our first one, which had been stolen by our slimeball rival, Raul DaSilva.

I was under orders from Allan Tanner, our race engineer, to relax and prepare mentally for the big Miami oval. We were sitting third in the championship and, with a bit of luck, still had a shot at the title. My homework consisted of computer races on one of Rick's laptops (crashed five times, best finish, eleventh) and long talks with Allan Tanner about race strategies and reacting to the unexpected. Allan had twenty years of experience in pro racing and when he talked, I listened. Above all, he stressed that I needed to focus—to stay cool under pressure. J.R. Reynolds listened in closely, adding his advice from decisions he'd made in the business world, which, he was beginning to see, wasn't much different than running a competitive race team.

Aunt Sophie and Susan Reynolds lived in the kitchen, conspiring together to create new and incredibly spicy versions of pasta dishes which we devoured daily. Caroline spent a lot of time in J.R.'s study, working on DynaSport's new secret project for this race. We went for long walks on the beach each night and had rambling discussions about art, music, movies, books, sports, politics, religion, the future of mankind, and what the purpose of it all might be. We both held strong opinions on things and didn't always agree, which only increased my interest. Once I had looked past her stunning natural beauty—not an easy task on a Florida beach at sunset— I discovered that Caroline Grant was a deep thinker with a strong desire to make a difference in the world. Beauty, brains, and a good heart were fast becoming an irresistible combination.

I also had time to catch up on my e-mails and to make phone calls home to Vancouver, British Columbia.

Our team had apparently also made the local papers, to the delight of Aunt Sophie. My dad, the accountant, was in the middle of some huge audit for one of his clients and wouldn't be able to get down to Florida for the final race. Neither would Rick and Caroline's folks, but I did learn that they had already booked a restaurant and expected all of us back home shortly for a victory party. I liked their confidence.

One of the e-mails was from Stefan Veilleux, the fourth-place driver in the championship. At maybe five foot two with curly black hair and an impish grin, Stefan looked like an elf or a hobbit. Strapped into a race car, however, he was a fast and tough competitor, and we had quickly become close friends. It was when Stefan had gone home to visit his family at their estate in Bordeaux, France, that he had accessed our website. His e-mail message was written in his typical wounded English, and it indicated when he was arriving in Miami to rejoin his team. J.R. suggested that I take his mint '64 Chevy Impala convertible, pick Stefan up at the airport, and bring him back to the beach house for dinner. It proved to be a great idea. I really only knew Stefan as a racing driver, but during the course of the evening I found out a good deal more.

The Veilleux family went back seven generations in the rich French wine country around Avignon. They owned several thousand acres of vineyards, the local soccer team, and three car dealerships. Clearly, Stefan's family had the funds to support his racing career as far as he wanted to go. Stefan's father had been a racing driver himself, specializing in long-distance European sports car races. About twenty-five years ago, his dad had been part of a team that won the biggest sports car race of them all, the 24 Hours of Le Mans, in a factory Porsche. The next day, he retired to look after his businesses and young family. It didn't take Stefan long to get the bug. At ten he started racing karts, won several local and national titles by the age of fourteen, and became the youngest ever Formula Renault champion at seventeen. From there he had gone on to two years of Formula Three in Europe and in England, but he had only mixed success with unreliable cars. That had brought him over to the North American Formula Atlantic Series last year for a fresh start. As he was now in the hunt for the championship, it seemed like a very good career move.

Nearing midnight, Caroline and I drove Stefan an hour south to the Glades, a sprawling hotel and convention center complex, right across the highway from the Homestead Motorsport Park. Blocks of rooms had been set aside for all of the Atlantic teams, including us. We eventually found Stefan's crew on the hotel's tennis courts playing soccer in the dark with a fluorescent beach ball. After a quick round of introductions, we declined an offer to join in, and started back for West Palm Beach.

On the way, Caroline and I got into another of our meaning-of-life discussions, missed our freeway turnoff, and got thoroughly lost for an hour. By the time we had backtracked, found the right highway exit, and finally returned to the Reynolds' home, it was well into the early hours of the morning. Under a moonless night, the house was completely dark.

"We are so late, Eddie. Be really quiet," Caroline whispered as she fumbled for her house keys.

We padded silently around to the back of the house, and Caroline gently unlocked the sliding deck door.

"Don't turn on the lights," I warned.

I didn't want to disturb anyone and risk the ferocious teasing that would quickly follow. Caroline and I had been seeing a lot of each other, and in the eyes of the crew we had "a thing" going on. They delighted in pointing out how obvious our attraction had become. We crept into the still, silent house, gently slid the door closed and locked it. Slowly we began to feel our way toward the staircase through the blackness. Abruptly Caroline stopped.

"Eddie, do you have my purse?" she whispered.

I considered the question for a moment. "No. It doesn't go with my shoes."

"Very clever. Could you go back to the car and get it for me? Please?"

No problem, I thought. I unlocked the sliding door, closed it silently behind me, went back out to the Chevy, found the purse on the floor, and returned to the house. I slid back the door, slipped inside again, and locked it. The I stopped. The house remained dark and still.

But it wasn't quite silent anymore.

Chapter 4

Midnight Tour

The sound of heavy breathing was very close. Something big was ahead of me in the inky darkness—something with warm, moist breath. I wondered if the stories about alligator attacks in Florida homes were true.

"Caroline?" I whispered.

Nothing.

Something moved, and I took a step back against the glass door, feeling for the latch or a light switch. I was nowhere near either, and Caroline wasn't answering. I was blind and backed into a corner. I had to figure out what to do next—and quickly. I decided to speak up.

"Who's there?" I said with more confidence than I felt. Again, nothing—just the regular, heavy breathing against the pounding of my increasing heartbeat.

The mind does strange things when you're scared in the dark. I considered letting whatever was out there know that I wasn't about to curl up and die quietly. After all, I was armed. Only I knew that my weapon was a red leather purse. Then a scene from an old British war movie popped into my head, where a soldier was on night watch and sensed an enemy somewhere out there in the blackness. I remembered the standard war movie line and decided to use it.

"Who goes there? Friend or foe?" I said in my best honor guard voice.

Nothing happened for a moment. Then something moved swiftly toward me through the blackness. My heart skipped a beat as jaws closed around my left wrist. My purse hand! Having lost the use of my weapon, I lunged across with my right hand, and grabbed smooth skin. An animal had my arm, but it didn't feel anything like an alligator. Plus, I still had my left hand. I felt around the jaws more slowly, finding two ears and a cold wet nose. I breathed a heavy sigh of relief. It was Clarence, my pal. Ever loyal, he had waited up for us, which was nice. Nice for a few seconds...until I realized that he wasn't letting go. Worse yet, I realized with mounting horror that I had said Clarence's special word, "friend," which to his Labrador retriever brain meant only one thing.

We were going on the tour.

Clarence didn't seem to be bothered by the dark, and we moved a lot more quickly this time. He must have figured that I only needed the refresher tour. He pulled me through the kitchen, but not before I had bounced off a wall, knocked a vase of flowers off the counter, and stubbed my toe on something big. So much for being quiet. Limping and desperately looking for a light switch as we exited the kitchen, I saw the outline of a floor lamp and lunged for it. But Clarence yanked me sideways at the last second, which sent the lamp crashing to the floor. We accelerated into the living room, picking up the pace toward the front door. Something whacked me hard in the middle of both shins, and I went right over it, face first to the floor.

Then the lights came on.

Holding a baseball bat, John Reynolds stood with Caroline and Susan at the top of the stairs. He was soon joined by Allan and Sophie. Alfie scampered down the stairs, barked once in clear disapproval of Clarence, and then placed his paw on top of my outstretched arm and howled. The intruder was down. Clarence finally released my wrist and sat quietly next to me, panting and smiling up at J.R. I looked behind me and saw the shattered flower vase, the broken lamp, and the large redwood coffee table that had finally done me in.

"Good morning, boys!" J.R. announced from the upstairs landing.

The Lads smiled. I wanted to disappear into the carpet. Everyone took in the trail of destruction for a few seconds, and then the laughter started. Caroline even snapped pictures from the balcony. Clarence was banished to the outside deck in disgrace, while I limped quietly off to Alfie's room, grateful to have escaped the same judgment.

Chapter 5

Murphy's Law

By Wednesday morning of race week, Rick and Herb were back from Orlando with two new wings specially built for the Miami oval. My scraped shins were healing nicely. We loaded up for the short drive south to Homestead and registered at the Glades hotel complex. Then it was over to the track.

The Homestead Miami Speedway was designed to be one of the finest racing facilities in North America, maybe even in the world, and they got it right. It's a fantastic complex, with everything a race team or spectator could ask for. We would be racing on the big one-and-a-half-mile oval, which also includes a road course inside of it. Over 65,000 people can take in the action from grandstands, private corporate boxes, small parks, or the infield. The entire place is state of the art—spotlessly clean and ultra professional.

We had come a very long way from the mud and gravel at our first Trans-Am race only a few months before.

This time the Atlantic teams wouldn't be the supporting event to the Champ Cars or to anyone else. The North American Formula Atlantic Championship would be decided right here, this weekend, and we were the main event. J.R. had reserved a pit suite for us in the center of the infield, and the one we were assigned was easily the best pit garage I'd ever seen. It was almost the size of a real race shop, with a double overhead door, gleaming tile floor, stainless-steel workbenches, air conditioning, a complete private

bathroom, galley kitchen, and an office. There was more than enough room to move everything out of our trailer and into the pit garage. We could set up shop and really have room to work. Herb fell in love instantly and announced that he was moving in. Most of the Atlantic teams had also reserved pit garages.

All except Raul DaSilva's Ascension Motorsports outfit. Their two huge transporters and four motor homes were in the pit area, but they had chosen to set up well away from the other teams' garages. I hadn't seen a trace of Raul at the track or anywhere else, which was odd. He was sitting in second place in the championship, going into this final race, and was considered a title contender. The guy who was in first place, Kurt Heinrich, had been Raul's teammate until he made the mistake of winning more races than his boss. Mr. DaSilva had fired Kurt after the last race, which effectively now made Raul the championship favorite. I was right behind Raul in third place, followed by Stefan Veilleux in fourth. Less than four points separated the three of us. Unless Raul, Stefan, and I all failed to finish this final race, it was certain that one of us would take the championship.

With a shot at the title, we were going to make sure that everything on our car had been checked and rechecked. The rest of that day and all of Thursday and Friday were spent setting up the garage and completely stripping down our Swift Formula Atlantic car. Under Allan's direction we carefully removed every piece on the car, until all that remained was a black tub on waist-high work stands. Allan then began checking every nut, bolt, and wire. Rick fine-tuned his race data acquisition system and Herb had a fresh engine from Cosworth and a new gearbox ready to install.

"All of this preparation is our tribute to one of the great minds of our time," Allan announced as he removed the right front brake assembly.

All of us looked at him vacantly except J.R., who got it and smiled.

"I believe that Allan is referring to Mr. Murphy and his famous law," J.R. stated.

We were still lost.

"It's a simple law and especially important to remember when you are working with things that are dangerous if they break," Allan explained. "Like aircraft or space shuttles. Or racing cars."

J.R. nodded in agreement. "Mr. Murphy famously said, 'If something can go wrong, it will.' So you're smart to check everything twice and replace anything that looks like it could fail...because it probably will."

Rick nodded and offered his own version. "Just like computer programmers say, 'Garbage in, garbage out.'"

"Or, 'If you fail to prepare, prepare to fail,'" Caroline added.

Everyone considered these pearls of wisdom for a few moments.

Then it was Herb's turn. "OK, how about this: 'A chirping bird is better than a barfing cat.' I just made that one up...think about it," he announced with pride as he left the workshop for the trailer.

There was a long silence as we all looked at each other blankly and then went back to work, trying to work out how barfing cats applied to preparing our race car. What was clear, however, was that with the final race and a championship on the line, nothing would be left to chance. Or to Murphy's Law.

Chapter 6

Turn Left

Aside from a dozen or so laps in open
practice on Saturday morning to
break in the fresh engine, I hadn't yet
pushed the Swift hard. I was anxious
to see just how much speed it had.
Everything that could break on the car had been dou-
ble-checked, rebuilt, or replaced with new parts. We
were as ready as we were going to be. Saturday afternoon was the practice session. Allan's plan was to use
it to get as much data for Rick's computer as possible,
rather than to try and set a fast time right away. We
would save that for the second qualifying session.

The Homestead Miami oval is similar to the
Milwaukee track, with two straights connected by
four ninety-degree corners at each end and six
degrees of banking in the turns and thick concrete
walls. The big difference is that, at 1.5 miles, a lap at

Miami is a lot longer and faster than at the Milwaukee Mile. The outright lap record is held by a Champ Car, which had rocketed around in under 25 seconds. This weekend's race would be the first time that Formula Atlantic cars had run here. Allan figured that a lap in the low to mid 30-second range at an average speed of about 170 miles per hour would be right up there.

In order to run fast on a big oval, we spent a lot of time setting up the Swift's chassis. As you're always turning to the left, it's vital to adjust the car so that it wants to go that way naturally. This involves tweaking the steering, springs, shocks, wings, and tire pressures to the point where the car is really only happy turning left. This is a good thing for an oval, as turning right anywhere at those speeds would be instantly expensive—and painful.

The Swift was fitted with one of Rick's new wings, which had its aerodynamics worked out on his computer model and then had been tested in a wind tunnel earlier in the week. He was convinced that this design was even better than his original, which had been stolen at the last race by Raul DaSilva's thugs.

Three laps into the practice session, I knew he was right. The Swift streaked around the Miami oval almost as if it were on rails—smooth and stable. I was quickly lapping in the thirty-four-second range with lots left in reserve. But Allan came on the radio with instructions to stay at that pace and just put in the laps to allow the data sensors to collect as much information as possible. Rick and Allan would upload and analyze all the information they were collecting. They would then use the info to build a final setup for the second qualifying session later that afternoon. So I stayed out and comfortably reeled off the laps, resisting the temptation to race a few of the faster cars as I let them pass. The one guy I really wanted to go with was Raul DaSilva, but I never once saw his bright yellow car. Either he had some sort of major mechanical problem or he was saving it all for qualifying.

I stayed out for all of the forty-five-minute session. Then I brought the Swift back into our garage. Rick plugged a data cable into the nose of the car and began retrieving the information from the onboard sensors into his laptop for analysis. Herb and Allan stripped the bodywork away and raised the car up on stands. Then they began the process of going over everything again. There were two hours until the last qualifying session—lots of time for final checks and to make any fine adjustments.

As the temperature was climbing well into the eighties under a cloudless sky, I went straight to the motor home and gratefully got out of my triple-layer driving suit. To keep J.R. happy, I changed into a pair of DynaSport hiking shorts and a DynaSport golf shirt. Then I grabbed a pair of DynaSport cycling sunglasses and topped it off with a DynaSport baseball hat. I waved at Sophie and Caroline, who were lounging under a large umbrella on the roof, and set off down the pit area to see what everyone else was up to.

As usual, most of the pit garages housed well-prepared teams where the race crews quietly went about their business. The few who were less prepared were easy to spot as their cars were in pieces, tools were strewn across the floor, and nobody seemed to know

what to do next. It was a strong reminder of how fortunate I was to have a talented and professional crew. I was especially interested in what was going on with Raul DaSilva, who had yet to make an appearance on the track or in the pits. His team had set up well away from the other team garages. They had used their transporters and motor homes to form a large square with the inside covered by white awnings and tents. It looked like a top-secret lunar base.

I should have gone back to our own garage, but curiosity got the better of me. I really wanted to know what exactly could be going on inside that compound. I passed the garage area and walked casually down the pit lane until I was close enough to hear the familiar sounds of crewmen working on race cars. DaSilva's four team cars were in there being prepared for qualifying, but I could see nothing. I was about to slip behind the transporter to see if I could get a look inside the compound when I glanced over my shoulder to see a gleaming black Porsche Carrera pull up behind me and switch off. It was Kurt Heinrich's car. Kurt was Raul's ex-teammate, who'd been fired for not blocking well enough to help Raul win the last two races. Kurt had gone back to Germany; apparently he'd lost his Porsche as well as his job. Out stepped Raul himself, in a perfectly tailored cream silk suit and white silk shirt. I was ready for a blast from him accusing me of trespassing, but instead he was all smiles and full of charm.

"Stewart!" he exclaimed with his arms open wide as if we were long lost brothers. "How are you?"

"Hi, Raul. I was just—"

Raul interrupted me with upheld palms.

"You were stopping by to say hello, no? Excellent! I have just returned from Brazil and was planning to find you anyway. So, how is your fast red car?"

"Not bad at all. I think we'll be up there on race day."

Raul nodded in agreement.

"I think you will also. You have come far in a very short time. I may have underestimated you, Stewart. Your win in Toronto was well deserved."

That was about the last thing I expected to hear from Raul DaSilva—the guy who had stolen our wing in Toronto; ordered Kurt, his second driver, to take me out of the race; and almost put me in the wall himself. Now here he was, Mr. Friendly, leaning on his shiny new Porsche, admitting that he might have been wrong, and telling me what a great driver I was. Maybe he'd fallen on his head in Brazil.

Raul nodded toward his enclosed pit and winked. "Come. Let me show you inside. I think that you will be impressed."

Chapter 7

Drawing the Line

Curiosity pushed aside my better judgment. I followed Raul to the side of the transporter, where he unzipped one of the tent walls. We stepped inside. It was a huge area—as bright and humid as a greenhouse, but the air was kept comfortably cool by the air conditioners that hummed in the background. I counted twelve crewmen, all in their crisp black and yellow Ascension Motorsports uniforms, silently preparing four spotless Atlantic cars, which sat on fresh green carpets. Two of the cars were bright yellow and had Raul's name in huge letters, with his trademark red lightning bolts on the sides. The other two were pure black with yellow wings, and they carried the name of Raul's new second driver, Hiro Tanaka. Massive tool chests, compressed-air lines, and stainless-steel worktables ringed the work space.

Raul surveyed the operation with pride.

"Now, this is a professional race team, Stewart—the best mechanics and engineers, a complete spare car, and a crew of four for each driver. Fresh engines, gearboxes, and the latest computerized setup equipment. Here a driver has everything he needs to win."

It was definitely impressive, but I still felt uneasy, as if I'd let myself be sucked into a place that I knew I should stay away from. Raul glanced at his gold Rolex watch.

"Ah, time for lunch. You must join me," he stated.

"Actually, Raul, I have to be getting back to our garage."

"But you have two hours until qualifying. I assure

you that lunch with me is as good as any four-star restaurant. Besides, there is a matter that I wish to discuss with you. Join me. Please."

Please? Raul DaSilva actually used the word "please" in a conversation. Something had changed and I decided that I had an hour to spare in order to find out what it was.

He was right about lunch. We were served inside his palatial motor home by his personal chef, who prepared broiled fresh fish and steamed vegetables, followed by chocolate mousse. Throughout the meal Raul talked nonstop about himself (his favorite subject), providing details of his early days racing karts, then Formula Ford in England and his Formula Three Championship last year in Brazil. He was on an ambitious timetable, which he figured would take him into Champ Cars and then into Formula One over the next three years. Finishing dessert, we sat back over cups of rich Colombian coffee.

"So, did I not tell you that lunch would be superb?" he asked with pride.

I had to agree. "You did and it was."

Raul excused himself, went into one of the back rooms of the motor home and returned with a black leather case. He sat down, leaned forward, and fixed me with his small, dark eyes.

"I am pleased that you enjoyed lunch. It is an example of the way I do my business, and the way that I go motor racing—only the best."

I decided that this was as good a moment as any to see where he was coming from. His charm and grace might have convinced the public, but I'd seen this guy at work before and I wasn't ready to buy the new Raul. I had no reason to trust DaSilva. Still, he had said there was something he wanted to discuss with me. Maybe it was the stolen wing incident. I decided to find out.

"Let me ask you something, Raul. Your desire to have only the best—how far does that go?"

He wrinkled his dark brow and seemed puzzled.

"How far? Money is not a problem, Stewart, I assure you. I can easily afford to buy the best equipment and the best people, if that is what you mean."

It was my turn to lean forward and make meaningful eye contact.

"No, not exactly. What I'm wondering is, outside of the money, how far would you go to get an advantage? Where do you draw the line?"

He sat back and considered the question.

"Draw the line? What a strange expression. I am my own man, Stewart. I make my own way in the world. I am not bound by the rules or limits of others. There is no 'line,' as you put it. When I want something I find a way to get it."

It was time to be direct. "So, is that what happened to our wing in Toronto? You found a way?"

Raul's eyes narrowed as he tensed in his chair. It appeared that I had touched a nerve.

"Yes, the matter of your wing. Apparently two of my crewmen removed it from your trailer, repainted it, and fitted it to my car for the race. They told me that they had worked all night constructing it for me, based upon your design. They did not. I only learned the truth after the Toronto race. I fired them on the spot—more coffee?"

I considered this version of events as his chef brought us fresh cups of steaming coffee. Raul, the innocent bystander? It didn't fit with what Heinrich had told me, it didn't fit with Raul's actions during the Toronto race, and it didn't fit with what I knew of his character. What did fit was that he was lying. I was learning how to tell when DaSilva was lying. His lips moved.

"So, what happened to it?" I asked.

Raul's smile returned but this time it was the hawk grin that I'd seen before, the cold look of the predator. The charm had been stripped away. This was the guy I was used to. He placed the black leather case on the table, unzipped it, and removed two thick, white envelopes. He pushed the first one across the table to me.

"The wing is on my car. Let us agree that how it got there will remain between you and me at this table. And I am told that your team now has a new design, so it is old business, no? But I am prepared to offer you something for, shall we say, your understanding. The contents of that envelope will do that, I believe."

I picked up the envelope, opened it, and counted twenty fresh $1,000 bills. It was more than enough to pay for the wing. The rest was obviously for me to keep my mouth shut. I glanced up at Raul for a moment and then across to the second envelope, which was even thicker. Raul followed my gaze. I placed the first envelope next to me and sat back.

I should have walked, right then. But now I was even more curious than before. I decided to stay quiet, to play along a bit to see where, and how far, this would go—and to find out what was in that second envelope. Raul smiled with satisfaction.

"Good. Let us say no more of this wing business. That is the past. Let us talk now of the future, Stewart. Your future."

"I'm listening," I said. Raul DaSilva had my undivided attention.

Chapter 8

The Price

Raul spoke rapidly, his excitement growing as he moved closer to what I sensed was the real reason for this lunch meeting. I picked up the first envelope again, fingered the bills inside, looked up, and listened patiently.

"Going into this last race, I am second in the Atlantic Championship, Stewart. I intend to win it on Sunday. My men are this moment finishing modifications to my car, which will…which will give me an advantage. I have fired Heinrich, so that takes care of the series points leader. Stefan Veilleux is fast on road courses, but he does not do as well on the ovals. I have brought Tanaka over from Japan as my new number two driver, and he will take care of Veilleux…and anyone else. All is in place, except for one thing. You, Eddie Stewart. You have proven to be very fast everywhere. I think that it will come down to us."

"You may be right," I agreed. "It should be a good race."

Raul stood, walked to one of the large bay windows of the motor home and watched his crew at work.

"Yes, a good race. And if you should win—what then? A nice trophy, a little money, some champagne, and then a long winter searching for someone to give you sponsorship money so that you can survive to race again next year. Perhaps DynaSport will stay on. But what if they do not? Just because you have won some races, or even a championship, do not think that you will suddenly have sponsors lined up at your door. Sponsors come and go, Stewart. And you do not have money of your own to continue. You could get nothing and be out of racing in a month."

He returned to his seat and continued. "You are a very talented driver, Stewart. We both know this. But to move up in this sport, you need more than talent. What you need behind you is a team that has no need for outside money, a team that has its own funds, a team that can always afford to provide you with the best."

"A team like yours?" I offered.

"Exactly! Four years ago, on my eighteenth birthday, I went with my father to the Banco Nacional in São Paulo and inherited more money than you can imagine. A week later I formed my racing team, Ascension Motorsports, in order to win championships—first in Brazil, then in England, and now in America. Make no mistake. This Sunday I will add the title of North American Formula Atlantic Champion to my list. And after I do, I will then move up to the next level, Champ Cars, and perhaps an entry for the Indianapolis 500 in the next year. And when I move up, Stewart, so does my teammate."

"So what exactly are you suggesting?" I opened the door for him—and he stepped right in.

"A partnership, Stewart! Something for us both. I need to win on Sunday, and you need a top car for next year. Why then should we not help each other? Help me to win on Sunday and I can promise you a bright future. Tanaka will be out and you will be in as my teammate next season, driving in the Champ Car World Series."

He slid the second, thicker envelope across the table. I picked it up, opened it, and fingered another bunch of crisp $1,000 bills. But this time I couldn't get an exact count. There were just too many. I guessed that there was over $50,000 in cash in there. It was certainly more money than I had ever seen.

I swallowed hard as Raul sat back confidently.

"There is $70,000 for you now, Eddie. Consider it as a retainer for your services next season. There will be another $70,000 waiting for you after you drop out of the race on Sunday. Simply pull off and tell your team that you have had an electrical problem. Such failures are common and difficult to trace. No one will question your retirement from the race.

"You will be out and Tanaka will keep Stefan out of my way. I have already taken steps to ensure that I will have the fastest car in the field. My path to the championship will be clear. And, after I win, you can leave the amateurs behind. We will announce that I am moving up to the Champ Car Series and that you are joining Ascension Motorsports for next year, as my teammate. I am quite serious, Eddie. Already, I have four new Lola Champ Cars ordered for next season. Two of them and six crewmen can be yours, with a base salary of $250,000, plus whatever you win. We will race Champ Cars together next year in Australia, Mexico, Canada, and all over America. And then in a year or two…on to Formula One. Think of it!"

I did think of it. I thought hard. I shouldn't have, but I had to. Instead of getting up and leaving, it suddenly became all too easy to put aside my conscience and think about the cash plus a full-time ride in a new

Champ Car for next season. It might even lead to a chance at Formula One in a few years. In a sport where money often got you further than ability, any driver without a personal fortune, like me, would have to think hard about an offer like the one I'd just received.

I remained outwardly silent, but in my mind I was already behind the wheel of an 800-horsepower Lola, screaming around Road America and blasting through the turns in Surfers Paradise, Australia. I knew that Raul had the money to make that happen, and that I never would. Raul knew it, too. In fact, he was counting on it.

Raul rose from his chair, retrieved the two envelopes of cash, zipped them into the leather folder, and handed it to me.

"Come, let us walk together. You have much to think about."

We left the motor home and strolled back into the work area, where Raul's crewmen continued to prepare his cars. They were efficient, business-like, and professional, but above all, silent. There was none of the chatter or good-natured teasing that went on constantly in our garage. I noticed that no one even looked up as we walked around the cars. No one seemed to want to make eye contact. Maybe they just liked to keep to themselves…or maybe it was something else. It was almost as if they were hiding something. We made our way back through the tent wall, left the compound, and stopped next to the black Porsche.

"Ah, I almost forgot," Raul said as he fished the Porsche keys out of his suit pocket and tossed them over to me.

"Your company car. Come and see me after qualifying."

And with that, he disappeared back inside the walls of his pit.

I stood there with $90,000 in cash under my left arm, the Porsche keys in my right hand, and a huge decision to make. I knew the expression, "Everyone has their price"—that for enough money people will do just about anything—but I hadn't really believed it was true until that moment. I began to feel the tightening grip of a kind of fear that I hadn't experienced before. It wasn't the fear that every driver has of breaking his legs or being burned in a race car. This was stronger and came from somewhere much deeper. It was the kind of fear that makes your breath short, that dries out your mouth, that makes your palms sweat, and makes your heartbeat hammer inside your head.

I turned and walked slowly back toward our garage. What was at risk was more than pain and injury. It was my character—who I was and what I stood for. Did my loyalty, honesty, and integrity have a price? Was cash, a season in Champ Cars, a six-figure salary, and this gleaming black Porsche enough? Was that my price? I understood then why I was afraid. I was about to find out.

Chapter 9

Out of the Zone

I t was a short walk back to our garage. I took my time, trying to sort out all that had just happened. On a simple level, I'd just been offered a huge contract with a top team. There was no doubt that DaSilva had the money, raw ambition, and talent to buy his way to the top. And I had to admit that he was right about my future—that if I couldn't find enough sponsorship money, my chances of moving up the pro racing ladder were slim.

I reached our pit garage, but instead of going in I went straight to our Dodge tow truck and locked the black leather folder in the glove compartment. Then I went over to the motor home, told Sophie and Caroline that I was going to relax before qualifying, lay down in the back bedroom, and locked the door. For the next hour I tried without success to sort out my thoughts and decide what I should do.

Finally, Herb picked the lock and barged in.

"Wake up, racer boy!" he yelled, clapping his hands.

"I am awake," I muttered.

"Well, suit up! In ten minutes I'm going to watch you put our car on the pole."

I went through the familiar process of fireproofing myself by pulling on flameproof socks and under-wear. I stepped into my three-layer quilted driving suit, laced up my custom driving shoes, and grabbed my helmet bag. I walked into the pit garage to find the Swift ready and waiting.

There was a lot of excited chatter from everyone. Rick was especially pumped about the changes he had made based upon his data acquisition system. They knew they'd built a fast car, and I knew that they had confidence in me to get the most out of it. Normally I would have shared that confidence, but I found that I couldn't.

I said nothing and avoided eye contact. Silently I pulled on my hood and helmet, and slid down and into the Swift. For the first time ever I felt awkward and strangely out of place with my crew, some of whom were my best friends. I couldn't stop thinking about Raul's offer, about that folder locked in the truck, and about bailing on my friends to advance my

career. And I couldn't stand to be around them with those thoughts racing through my head. I felt like a traitor.

As usual, Herb helped me buckle up the six-point safety harness. Then Allan knelt down beside the car to test the onboard radio.

"Receiving me, Edward?" he smiled.

I flipped down the helmet visor to hide my eyes and pressed the small yellow transmit button on the steering wheel.

"Sounds fine. Fire it up and let's go," I snapped.

My tone of voice caused Allan to pause for a moment, but then he stood and nodded to Herb and

Rick at the back of the car. They spun the starter and the engine instantly exploded to life. They gave me a push on the rear wing. I jammed the gear lever into first and snapped the Swift hard out of our pit garage into the pit lane.

I was the first car to get in line for the fast-group qualifying session. They waved me out right away. Atlantic qualifying on the oval was done one car at a time, with each driver getting one warm-up lap plus four more to set a time. I took it easy in the warm-up lap to make sure that everything was up to operating temperature, especially the tires.

When I passed the pits to start my first timed lap, Allan came on the radio.

"How does it feel, Edward?"

"Fine."

"OK. Build some speed."

The car had felt strong in the earlier session; it was better now. The crew's fine-tuning, based upon Rick's computer data, had given me a race car that was immediately fast and stable just about anywhere I chose to put it on the track. My first lap was almost at full race speed. But I was having trouble focusing and keeping it smooth. The car felt like it was out ahead of me all the time and I was fighting it, which was never a good sign.

I pushed harder on laps two and three, going deeper into the turns before lifting and looking for a faster cornering line. I needed to get down to a 33- or 32-second lap, which is what I'd need to start near the front. Starting my fourth and final qualifying lap, I was still looking for some speed. The last time I passed the pits, Herb was there holding the pit board with my time of 35.8. It was slow, and I knew that it wasn't the car. I was sure that my crew knew it, too.

I tried hard to concentrate. To go faster, I had to find the car's limits and then take it up there on every corner in a smooth, fluid rhythm. Rick called it "being in the zone." That was where I'd find the speed I knew this car was waiting to deliver.

Time for one more lap. I still couldn't find a fast rhythm, but I pushed hard anyway, hoping to force the speed to come. I buried the throttle for as long as I dared and desperately threw the car hard into each corner, but all I was doing was thrashing it around. I didn't feel any faster, and as I crossed the line to complete my four laps, Herb's pit board confirmed it with a 34.8. That time would put us nowhere near the front.

I angrily pulled the Swift into the pit lane, drove right past my waiting crew, blasted it into the garage, and killed the engine. I thought for a moment about making up some excuse to explain my lack of speed, but I didn't. Lying is hard work; I already had enough on my mind.

I unbuckled and threw off the safety harness. Then I yanked the radio cable out of the side of my helmet and climbed angrily out of the car as Rick, Herb, and Allan walked into the garage. They watched as I pulled off my gloves, helmet, and hood—and threw them into the car in frustration. I stared hard at the three of them.

"So?" I snapped.

Herb looked at his time sheets. "Well, you did a 34.82, which should qualify us somewhere near—"

"The middle. In other words, Rick, nowhere!"

There was an awkward silence.

"Maybe it's my new wing, Eddie," Rick offered quietly. "We could try the other one if you want."

I shook my head and glared at the floor.

"No, Rick. Leave it," Allan said, eyeing me narrowly. "There's nothing wrong with the wing."

Chapter 10

The Cost

I have never understood why British people instinctively believe that any problem known to civilization can be solved over a cup of tea. I sat in the motor home kitchen while Allan went through his precise ritual of brewing Earl Grey tea, his favorite. Having been in the race engineering business for over twenty years at every level, from karts to Formula One, Allan Tanner knew a few things about race cars, and about race drivers. We had managed to talk him into working with us just after he quit DaSilva's team. He had rapidly brought the raw talent on our young team together. He could probably have had his pick of race teams anywhere in the world. We were lucky to have him.

"It's all about timing, Edward. Timing is everything. Observe closely. You must be sure to warm the pot...then put in the tea leaves—never those dreadful bags. Then, and only then, you pour in the water…when it's boiling, so that it attacks the leaves and draws out their full flavor."

He poured and then brought two mugs of Earl Grey over to the table, smiling with satisfaction as he savored the aroma. I wasn't big on tea, but with a little milk and sugar it was passable—and certainly safer than Herb's coffee. Allan sipped his with closed eyes, and sat back with satisfaction. I stirred mine and, sitting in awkward silence, stared at the spoon.

"Not your best day, Edward," he said.

It wasn't a question, just a blunt statement of fact. I was at least two seconds off the pace in a car that should have been on the front row—and we both knew it. There was no point in pretending that something was wrong with the Swift. I was the problem. We both knew it. I stared at my spoon for a while and then looked up and nodded.

"I didn't focus."

"You *couldn't* focus," he corrected me. "You were afraid out there."

I started to protest but he held up his hand.

"Don't, Edward. I've worked with too many drivers and I've seen it before. Fear is nothing to be ashamed about. Any racing driver who tells you that he's never been afraid is lying or he's a fool. It happens to everyone, especially at a fast track like this with no room for error. This place can hurt you, no mistake. But you've been gifted with as much natural talent as I've seen in a long time, Edward. And up to this afternoon, you've also had the mental toughness to overcome your fear and to focus on using it. What happened to change that?"

I pushed my mug aside.

"It's not the speed or the chance of getting hurt; I've come to terms with that. It's not that kind of fear. It's something else. I've had an offer to drive for another team."

Allan nodded to himself, as if confirming something he had suspected.

"Well, that is going to happen if you're quick, Edward, and you are. Other teams are always looking for talented drivers. Don't let that upset you. What's the offer?"

I laid it out in detail for him—the cash, the salary, the Porsche, and next season in the Champ Car Series. Everything, except who it was from and what the catch was.

Allan raised his eyebrows. "That's an extremely attractive offer. Certainly well beyond what this team could provide. Friendships aside, you do have to think about your future. It is a business after all," he said.

I *had* thought about my future and what it would be like if I accepted Raul's deal. I was past the initial thrill of seeing myself in a Champ Car. What came to my mind now was Kurt Heinrich. Kurt was a very talented driver and had probably worked under the same conditions that I had been offered. Follow orders, keep your mouth shut, and do whatever it takes to help Raul win. In return, I would get to race as a well-paid professional in a top international series. I remembered what Kurt had told me before he left—about selling out to Raul and about how he finally couldn't live with himself anymore. Everyone has their price and Kurt had found out what his was.

I was beginning to understand that it wasn't so much a matter of price. It was really about *cost*. If I agreed to Raul's terms, I stood to gain what I had always dreamed about—a paid ride with a big-budget professional team that could really launch my career. But if I accepted it, I'd also have to live each day with what that had cost me—knowing I hadn't found the strength to walk away, and knowing I'd done the easy thing instead of the right thing.

I thought about what it would feel like to throw the race away on Sunday. I thought of my friends and the lies I would have to tell Rick, Herb, Aunt Sophie, Allan, J.R. Reynolds—and especially Caroline. I thought about how it would feel to cheat, lie about it, and then just walk away after all they'd done for me. And I thought about what it would be like to live inside those lies every day—to deceive myself until I finally lost the ability to know what was right, or what the truth really was. Or who I was.

That was the price tag. That was what it would cost me.

I took a sip of my tea and Allan noticed that my hand was shaking.

"Edward, moving to the top level is a huge step. There's certainly more danger and a lot more pressure. And, having been there, I'd have to say it's a good deal less fun. So it's a bit scary. But this sounds like an excellent offer and you do have the ability. Do you doubt that?"

I shook my head.

"No Allan, I don't. I know that sounds pretty arrogant, doesn't it? It would be very tough, but I know that I could compete. That's not what scares me. It's what I'd have to do to get there."

Then I told him the rest. All of it—the dark side, including who was behind the offer and what the conditions and expectations were. Allan listened to it all patiently and didn't look surprised when he heard Raul DaSilva's name. He didn't say anything right away, just got up from the table, took the two mugs, rinsed them, and placed them in the sink. Then he paused before walking out the door.

"I said earlier that I had confidence in your ability, Edward. And I do. I also have confidence in your character. You know what's right here, and what to do next. That's the difference between you and people like Raul."

Allan left and closed the door quietly. I was tired of sitting and thinking about it. The time had come to make my decision.

Chapter 11

Decision Time

I left the motor home, then retrieved the leather case from the tow truck. I walked briskly down the pit lane to DaSilva's compound and asked one of his crewmen to find him for me. I waited outside the tented walls, leaning against the open window of the gleaming black Porsche, turning the keys over in my hand. Raul arrived in less than a minute, smiling broadly. If I had needed a final reason to say no, he handed it to me right then.

"So, Stewart, we have a deal, no? What do you have to lose?"

There it was exactly. What did I have to lose? Everything that really mattered to me. My friends, my integrity, and my self respect. I looked at him for a while, not with awe or anger or caution anymore, but with something closer to pity. I was surprised to find myself almost feeling sorry for this guy, whose only way of achieving success was to buy it or steal it. For the first time I looked past the money and saw Raul DaSilva as a small, friendless, and desperate man—a man who knew the price of everything and the value of nothing.

I unzipped the leather folder, put the Porsche keys inside, and handed it back to him.

"Can't do it, Raul. It's not in me. This whole deal is just wrong."

He snatched the folder from my hand. Then the volcano that was always boiling inside Raul DaSilva shattered his plastic smile, revealing his most honest emotion—explosive rage.

"Wrong? Do you think we are in Sunday school, Stewart? There is no right and wrong! There is only what you must do to win! Take what you want! Grow up and be a man!" he screamed.

I almost rose to the insult, but I found that I just didn't need to anymore. I had met Raul on his turf, seen him for what he was, and refused to become the same thing. That was enough.

"Listen, Raul. If I get anywhere in this sport it's going to be because I've earned it. Not because I sold out."

Raul flung the leather case into the Porsche in fury.

"You will regret this, Stewart!"

"Somehow I doubt it, Raul," I replied as I turned and walked back to our garage, feeling stronger with every step.

Late that afternoon I locked up the garage and took everyone out for dinner. It was a chance for me to apologize for being a jerk, and to let them in on Raul's offer. They listened in stony silence and shook their heads in disgust. In my confusion, I hadn't stopped to consider how DaSilva could have used his promise to remove me as a challenger and then simply walk away from the deal once he had the championship, leaving me with nothing. Sophie had seen that immediately. When I finally understood that side, I realized how close I'd come to losing more than just a race.

With a quiet word to Caroline, J.R. and Susan Reynolds left to pick up some friends at the airport. They had flown them in for this race—a great way for J.R. to entertain some of DynaSport's major business clients.

Over dessert, the discussion quickly turned from DaSilva's latest plot to our race strategy for tomorrow. The bad news was that my poor qualifying performance had placed us in the middle of the pack, fourteenth of twenty-eight cars. It would be a tall order to haul myself up to the front. The good news was that we still had a very fast car. Provided that I got my act together on Sunday, we had a shot.

Chapter 12

The Pool Show

Caroline and Sophie had made plans for the evening. Rick, Herb, and Allan were heading back to the shop to finish up some preparations. It had been a long, stressful day. I decided to turn in early and rest up for tomorrow.

It wasn't just another race. We were in the hunt for the Formula Atlantic Championship and I wanted to start fresh and ready. I was physically drained, but my brain had other ideas. After two hours of tossing and turning, I gave up and got dressed. I decided to go for a midnight stroll around the grounds of the Glades hotel complex.

It was the start of a truly bizarre evening.

It was a big race weekend and the laughter and music of fan parties spilled out of many of the rooms into the warm night air. The hotel ballroom was hosting a big and very loud wedding, which for some reason had a large number of accordion players. I walked through the patio gardens, past the tennis courts, through the lobby, and finally back outside again. The huge outdoor pool was brightly lit with underwater lights. Feeling hungry, I found a restaurant next to the pool, which was still open, and decided to stop for something to eat.

There were two levels to the restaurant. The poolside section was dim and deserted, but the lower level was open. I went down the stairs to find a large room with a solid glass wall that looked directly into the pool. Despite the hour, it was full of late-evening diners and I had to wait a few minutes until a table, near the piano player, became available.

I ordered a clubhouse sandwich and a milkshake, and peered through the thick glass into the giant aquarium as the floodlights played against the ripples in the water. The stillness of the scene was suddenly interrupted by a beautiful blonde girl in a red bathing suit who knifed into the water in a perfect dive and then glided gracefully to the surface. She left the pool, and then repeated three more dives to appreciative glances from everyone in the restaurant. She was very athletic and looked strangely familiar. I had a flashback to the diving I'd watched on TV at the Summer

Olympics last month, and I wondered if this was part of the hotel's usual evening entertainment.

That idea was shattered as something new blasted into the water like a meteor, sending large waves surging across the surface of the pool. It was a second female diver in a bright floral bathing suit and a pink bathing cap. She was easily three times the size of the first diver, and she quickly began to sink toward the bottom of the pool. Music and conversation in the restaurant stopped as people began to look alarmed. But the first diver soon reappeared, smoothly rescued her extra-large friend, and brought her to the surface. They left the pool but quickly returned in less than a minute, with the extra-large diver now wearing an orange life jacket. This midnight aquatic performance riveted everyone's attention on the glass wall. We all waited to see what would happen next.

What we got was something like synchronized swimming, although in the case of the XL swimmer it was closer to synchronized drowning. The athletic blonde girl was actually quite good as she gracefully slipped through the water. But her partner bobbed up and down like a large cork barrel. It was like watching the Little Mermaid and her pet whale. They did ballet moves, stuck their feet above the surface, and even tried unsuccessfully to build a pyramid. They were having a great time, completely unaware that a room full of people were watching their every move, cheering them on for a full fifteen minutes until they finally left the pool. I finished my sandwich and paid the bill. I was about to get up when people at the far end of the restaurant began to stand up and applaud.

Coming down the stairs into the restaurant in white bathrobes were our two swimmers. At first I couldn't see them clearly from across the room, but there was no mistaking that the XL lady led the way. She stopped on the staircase and seemed confused by the reception she was getting. Then someone laughed and pointed to the glass wall, and she covered her mouth in shock. Her beautiful, athletic partner was frozen in horror. As I was. Once they came down the staircase and entered the restaurant, it became clear that it wasn't the Little Mermaid and Moby Dick. It was Caroline and my Aunt Sophie.

Caroline looked like she wanted to crawl under a rock. But Sophie quickly warmed to the applause. She spread her arms wide and bowed gracefully to the audience. I crossed the restaurant and brought them both back to my table, where I ordered dessert for us all. Sophie thought the whole episode was hilarious, while Caroline slouched and hid behind the menu. The manager personally brought us large pieces of key lime pie, insisted it was on the house, and asked seriously if they could come back tomorrow. Caroline told him quietly that we had other plans.

Chapter 13

Trevor

I came back from a two-mile run early Sunday morning and watched the sun come up into a cloudless, deep blue sky. It was going to be another hot day, with track temperatures well over 100 degrees. I showered and then made the short drive over to our pit garage at Homestead Motorsport Park, where Sophie had prepared breakfast. I'd never seen that many pancakes in my life. Herb was in his glory.

Breakfast was washed down with gallons of Herb's "real" coffee, and I took a cup and strolled into the pit garage where I found Herb sitting alone on the floor next to the Swift. I stopped and smiled. Race day morning was an important time for Herb. Racing cars were a lot more than pieces of exotic machinery for him. When we used to race our Trans-Am Mustang, he would squeeze into it early on race day morning to have a quiet chat—just the two of them. Herb was much too big to slide into a Formula Atlantic car, so the next best thing was to sit on the floor next to it. He spoke to the Swift softly and patiently.

"OK, this is a big race. We could win a championship today. We've put you back together with all the best parts and you're tuned exactly right. You're ready. So run fast today…and don't hurt Eddie."

Then, as usual, Herb—the Man of Steel—bowed his head and was quiet.

While our garage was peaceful, there seemed to be a lot of new activity around our motor home, where a large white van had pulled up. J.R. and Susan Reynolds stepped out and went around to the back of the van, where a hydraulic ramp was lowered. Four kids came down the ramp and into our pit area, their eyes wide in wonder. Caroline came over and stood next to me, grinning with pride.

"Remember that special project J.R. had me working on? The one I told you I thought was generous? Well, here it is, Eddie. Just look at those faces," she said.

There were two guys and two girls, all about nine or ten years old. They were outfitted in blue and white DynaSport Motorsports jackets and ball caps. And all of them were in wheelchairs. As soon as they cleared the ramp, they used their strong arms to explore the pit area in excitement. From the look of their tiny legs, it was obvious that they were paralyzed from the waist down, either from birth or by accident.

A boy with freckles, thick glasses, and his hat on backwards, wheeled over and stopped at my feet. "Hey! You're Eddie Stewart."

I knelt down and we shook hands.

"Yes, I am. And who are you?"

"I'm Trevor, I'm nine, I'm from New Jersey, I love racing, and in my essay I—"

"Hold on, Trevor," I interrupted. "Your essay?"

"Yeah! Mr. Reynolds has this camp up in New York for paralyzed kids, and I've been going since I was five, and then he had this contest, and I entered, and I wrote this cool essay about you and the team, and so I won this trip 'cause I know like tons about racing! I know that you won the Pacific Northwest Formula Ford Championship, and that you raced a Mustang in the Trans-Am, and now you could win the Atlantic title."

"Man, you're pretty smart for a nine-year-old kid, Trevor," I said.

"I know," he replied, absently looking around the garage as if everyone told him that. Maybe they did. "Well, gotta go see the crew. Come on, Caroline!"

With Caroline in tow, Trevor zipped away toward the race car, where the other kids were already huddled around and talking with Allan, Herb, and Rick.

I looked over at J.R. and Susan Reynolds as they stood back and watched the scene with pure delight. They had started DynaSport in the early 1980s, building some of the first snowboards, and then progressing into skis, skiwear, and mountain bikes. J.R. had told me that in college he was a full-scholarship football player and had gone in the fourth round of the NFL draft. He was all set for a pro football career until he broke his neck on the third day of training camp.

That injury left him semi-paralyzed for three months and ended his football career. He eventually made a full recovery, but he never forgot the experience.

J.R. knew something of the fears and struggles these kids faced every day. This was one of the ways he had decided to make a difference, and now I understood what Caroline had meant when she described this as a generous project. Even though DynaSport was now an international company that did almost 300 million dollars' worth of business around the world each year, these kids were obviously among their most important clients. J.R. and Susan were truly great people, and I wondered why a day earlier my greed had almost resulted in leaving them behind for someone like DaSilva. It would have been a very expensive mistake.

Chapter 14

Ok to Be Third

By late morning, J.R. and his guests had set up on top of the pit garage. We were getting ready for the warm-up session, which would give us a chance to check our race setup. I had changed into my driving suit, which was the least comfortable outfit for a blistering Florida afternoon, and was strapped snugly into the Swift. Allan and I did our radio check.

"All right then, Edward. You're carrying a full fuel load. It may feel a bit sluggish compared to qualifying yesterday. Watch that it doesn't bottom out. No need to set a fast time. Just bed in the new brake pads and scrub this set of tires. Nice and easy."

I gave Allan a thumbs-up, and waited a moment until Herb spun the remote starter and fired the engine. With a quick check of the gauges to make sure that the oil pressure, water temperature, and fuel pressure were OK, I selected first gear, rolled out into the pit lane, and accelerated slowly onto the oval.

I took four laps to bring the car and myself up to speed. Unlike yesterday's qualifying run, my head was clear and I felt relaxed, comfortable, and focused. I was finally able to concentrate and sense what the car was doing. It was set up beautifully, carving each turn cleanly and pulling hard down the straights. As I got up to race speed, I noticed that the Swift cornered with just a hint of understeer, or push, just like it had when we raced at the Milwaukee Mile. It was a good setup for a fast oval because it allowed the front end to slide before the back. When the front end slid, I could regain control by easing off the gas slightly until the front tires bit again, which allowed the car to regain its line and exit the corner safely. What I didn't want was a car set up with oversteer or that was loose. Oversteer allowed the rear end of the car to slide first. If the back wheels stepped out in the middle of an oval corner, I'd be in the wall like that.

Rick's new rear-wing design was creating a ton of negative lift, or downforce, which pushed the car down onto the track, increasing traction and cornering speed without creating too much drag on the straights. The driving rhythm of acceleration, lift points, and turn in angles finally came. I was even able to brake into the corners with my left foot, while rolling smoothly off the throttle with my right. I finished the warm-up with a smile on my face. For the first time all weekend, I was hooked up with the car. I was in the zone.

Stefan Veilleux joined us for lunch on top of our pit garage and was an instant hit with our ten-year-old guests. Then Trevor the race expert wheeled over and talked to Stefan about race cars—in French. Stefan was hugely impressed.

"Eedie! This boy, Treevor. His French is simple but good. And he is so young. An amazement! So, your red car, she will be faster than fourteenth today?"

I chewed my sandwich and nodded. "Actually, there was nothing wrong with it yesterday. It was me. I just wasn't doing my job. Today will be different." Stefan was pleased.

"Good! I am missing you up front, Eedie. Raul is on pole and he is so fast! He does the 30-second lap yesterday. Can you believe this?"

I stopped chewing. I knew that Raul had qualified fastest and taken the pole. But I didn't know that he was down to 30 seconds. That was incredible. That was a decent Champ Car lap time at this track.

"Raul and his new boy, Tanaka, they are in front of me," Stefan continued. "I am not to liking this. They are the maniacs, I think. I have not the trust for them like it is for you. I am to starting from the tird place and—"

Caroline held up her hand and stopped him right there. We secretly loved listening to Stefan's struggles with English, but this was too much for her. She had to correct this one.

"Stefan, you can't be in *tird* place. It's third. T-h-i-r-d. Like three. You don't want to leave out the H."

Stefan shrugged.

"Tird? Thhhhird? It is the same, no?"

"No!" Caroline replied firmly. "Third is place three. You know—first, second, third. Like where you'll start the race today. 'Tird' means…something different…a lot different. Eddie will explain it."

Caroline has a college degree in art and I have one in communications, so it was obvious that they should look to me for guidance.

"Thank you so much, Caroline," I responded icily. "OK, let's see… Stefan, do you have a dog?"

"Ah, *oui*. Yes! At home in France I have the big black Bouvier dog. He is Muffy."

"Muffy? OK. Say you take Muffy out for a walk and he, uh…he does his business…he leaves behind a deposit…."

This wasn't going well. Stefan was even more

confused than before.

"Business? Deposit? Muffy does not do business. He does not go to the bank, Eedie."

Caroline called Trevor over and whispered into his ear for a few seconds. He cracked up but agreed to try, with the French he knew, to explain this delicate point of English language to Stefan. It took a few tries but we could certainly tell from Stefan's face when it finally clicked. He roared with laughter.

"Ha! I see! I am now very glad that I am to knowing this. Is OK to be the third. Not OK to be the tird!"

Chapter 15

Sir Edward

While the three preliminary races were going on, we met in the garage to go over strategy for our race.

The North American Atlantic Championship was a short but very competitive series, and while a number of different drivers had scored points over the last five races, no one had dominated. Usually, 10 points were awarded for a win, 8 for second, 6 for third, then 4, 2, and 1 down to sixth place. For this final race, however, the officials decided to make it more interesting by doubling the points to 20 for a win, 16 for second, 12 for third, and so on. Heading into the final, I had 18 points, Stefan had 16, and, with Kurt Heinrich now out of the series, Raul DaSilva was the title favorite with 20 points. Depending on where the three of us finished today, and with double-points awarded, any one of us could take the championship.

For me, it was pretty simple. I needed to finish in the top three and ahead of Raul to have any chance at the title. There was no point in sitting back and letting the race come to me. Starting  fourteenth in a field of twenty-eight cars, I would have to take some chances and be aggressive early, if I hoped to be in a position to win or finish on the podium. The race length was fifty laps, or about forty minutes. Our plan was to be running with the top six cars by half distance, and then use the final ten laps to try and fight through to the front.

Tire wear was going to a critical factor. Allan had impressed upon me the absolute importance of looking after my tires. Racing tires have a very short life on an oval, and if I pushed too hard early, I could easily use them up and be left without decent grip left at the end. The trick would be to balance speed with tire wear over the fifty laps.

At 2:30 p.m., the pit siren sounded. It was the signal for the teams to push their cars out on to the main straight and for the drivers to start strapping in. I grabbed my helmet, hood, and gloves and walked out to the bright red Swift with Caroline. I scanned the large crowd, which at an oval was all around the track. I glanced up to the top of the garages and waved to our cheering section, which consisted of J.R., Susan's kids, and Aunt Sophie. We reached the car and Caroline held my helmet and gloves while I put in my ear plugs and pulled on my fireproof hood and helmet. She brushed my hair away from my eyes and zipped up the collar of the driving suit.

"Ready for battle, Sir Edward?" she asked.

"Indeed. At your service, Lady Caroline," I replied gallantly.

She gave me a brilliant princess smile.

"Eddie, I want you to remember something today."

"Don't turn right?"

"Correct…and something else. Remember who you are. Go out there and be Fast Eddie Stewart today."

And with that, she handed me my gloves and kissed the front of my helmet. Then she left the track for our race pit. I stood there watching Caroline fade into the crowd until Herb came over, turned me around, and knocked on the side of my helmet.

"Hello? Hello? Earth to Eddie! Come on. It's show time!"

Chapter 16

Looking Good

With Herb's help I strapped in and tested radio communication with Allan. The starter held up the One Minute sign. We fired the engine and began rolling out behind the Ferrari pace car for the first of two warm-up laps, which were used to let everyone warm up their tires. Then the Ferrari pulled off and we began the final pace lap. The front-row cars, DaSilva and Tanaka, accelerated the field up to racing speed, while the rest of us back in the pack were required to hold position in our rows until Raul's pole car crossed the start-finish line to take the green flag.

The Swift felt strong and eager, but being stuck in the middle of the field, I had trouble seeing past the six rows of cars ahead to the front. I was trying to time my start with the moment the starter waved the green flag and maybe get a jump, but I just couldn't see well enough. Instead, I focused on the cars directly ahead and decided that when those guys hit the throttle, I would too. We rounded turn four and came out on to the main straight, anxious for the green. But we didn't get it. The starter didn't like the look of the field, which had become spread out and in a ragged formation, so he gave us a waved yellow flag instead of the green. We were going to have to go around and do it again.

The field was tighter on the second try. We finally got the green flag, which instantly unleashed a pack of twenty-eight howling Atlantic cars into the first turn. It's very risky to charge hard on the first lap of any race but it can be a perfect time to pick up places quickly when all the cars are sorting themselves out. I got a good start and immediately slashed down low into the first corner. Then I held a tight inside line through turn two, taking me out onto the back straight, past two cars, and up to twelveth place. I caught and passed another car in turn four and started the second lap running hard in eleventh. Allan came on the radio as I came off turn two and entered the back straight.

"Edward, do you read?"

"Go, Allan."

"Good start. Eleventh place. Build your speed."

It takes about three laps to get up to maximum speed on a fast oval. By lap five, the Swift was really hooked up. I had moved up another two places, and I was into a smooth driving rhythm. As I flashed past the pits, Herb's board confirmed that things were playing out nicely. He had written:

P9

L6

- 2

33.2

Ninth place, only six laps gone, two seconds and closing on the eighth-place car, and my last lap was in the low thirty-three second range, definitely fast for an Atlantic car at this track. I was into the top ten and moving up. I keyed the radio.

"Allan!"

"Go, Edward."

"Who's leading?"

"DaSilva. Tanaka, second. Veilleux, third. Bennedetto, fourth. You're catching the lead group."

"OK."

I stalked the eighth-place car for three laps before finally lining him up and passing him in turn three. That gave me some clear track and, for the first time, a distant look ahead. There were six cars in the lead group, all fairly close together—likely still feeling each other out at this early stage of the race.

I kept my foot hard into the throttle for the next five laps until I closed the distance to the sixth-place car. I used the draft from his slipstream to pick up more speed. Then I nipped out from behind and took him going into turn three. Herb's board confirmed that I was now part of the lead pack:

P6

L17

- 1

32.9

Sixth place, seventeen of fifty laps gone, a second behind the guy in front and lapping even faster than before. Three laps later, things improved again as the fifth-place car had a tire deflate and pulled off, handing me the place.

"Edward?"

"Go, Allan."

"Stay with the lead group now. Tires OK?

"Tires are good, Allan."

"Excellent. Pace yourself."

This was starting to look good. Very good.

Chapter 17

Tanaka

We were almost to the halfway point of the race and had achieved our first objective of getting into a position to challenge for the lead. Now it was important to think and drive a tactical race—to stay with the leaders for a while and move up if there was an opportunity. But, above all, I had to save the car for a charge to the front during the final few laps.

It had been a clean, green-flag race up to this point, but I wasn't surprised when we got a full-course yellow on lap twenty-five after someone slid up and brushed the wall in turn one. It wasn't a major wreck, but it did put us under yellow for three laps, which gave us a breather, and would also reduce tire wear slightly. I cruised around in third gear while the marshals cleaned some small pieces of wreckage from the track.

It was a good opportunity to map out a game plan for the final twenty-two laps. Raul was in first and seemed to be able to pull away, almost at will. He had enjoyed a healthy lead until the yellow allowed the field to close up right behind him. His new teammate, Hiro Tanaka, ran solidly in second. I'd never met him, but I knew that he had a reputation as a tough competitor in the Japanese Formula Nippon Series, and that he had European Formula Three experience. He was no rookie and would be a hard man to pass. Stefan Veilleux was third and having a good run, followed by the Italian, Elio Bennedetto. All four of the drivers in front of me were fast, professional, determined, and three of us had a chance at the title.

"Edward?"

"Go, Allan."

"Going green this lap. Set up a gap."

"OK."

I loved the gap. This was a restart tactic that Allan had explained to me weeks ago, but I hadn't had a chance to try it. Until now. It worked best if you were at the back of a group of cars waiting for the track to go from a single-file, no-passing, yellow condition back to a full race green condition. Usually, you waited for a restart by staying right up with the cars ahead until the green flag was shown, and then accelerating with them back up to racing speed. What Allan wanted me to try was to deliberately drop back from the cars ahead—to create a gap. When the track was about to go green again, the idea was to start accelerating into that gap just before the green flag was waved, and so get a jump on the guys ahead when it did go green. As with Earl Grey tea, timing was everything.

I slowed the Swift and let the four cars ahead pull away about ten car lengths.

"Gap is set, Allan."

"Good. Wait for my signal."

Allan had a perfect view of the starter's box from our race pit, while I was still back in traffic in the middle of turn four. As soon as he saw the starter pick up the green flag and get ready to wave it at the leader, Allan would radio me. If I started to close the gap too soon, I might pass someone under the yellow and be penalized—or even have to jam on the brakes and lose my advantage. Start to close the gap too late, and I would give up ten car lengths. But if it was timed exactly right, I could get an early jump on the restart.

As we came off turn four, I dropped down to second gear and got the call.

"Go! Go! Go!"

I nailed the throttle and the Swift lunged ahead, closing the gap rapidly to Bennedetto's fourth-place car. He had just begun to pick up speed with the lead group, but I was already accelerating hard through third—and then fourth—gear as we took the green flag from the starter. Allan had timed the restart perfectly. I went low to my left and pulled ahead of both Bennedetto and Stefan as we rushed three abreast toward turn one. I held the inside line through turn one and exited turn two solidly in third place, right behind Tanaka's black car. I tucked into his slipstream and thought about trying a low move going into turn three. But he had already seen me coming and moved down to block me.

We ran nose-to-tail for two laps, almost as one car—my front wing inches off his rear tire. I looked for a way past, going high and low. But every time I made a move, Tanaka matched it. I wasn't surprised. As I knew all too well, that was the job of Raul DaSilva's teammate. Tanaka was earning his money. My frustration was growing and I had missed the pit signals for the last few laps.

"Allan?"

"Go, Edward."

"Where are we?"

"Third place. Lap thirty-two. Eighteen to go. Be

patient."

"OK."

Patience was hard to come by when I knew that I was in a faster car and that I was being deliberately held up from catching the guy I had to beat. I stayed right with Tanaka on the next lap and took another run at him, low, going into turn one. To my surprise, I made it through easily into second place. Too easily, as it turned out. Tanaka then attacked from behind, actually bumping the back of my gearbox with the nose of his black car as we went into turn three. I had to lift for a few seconds to regain control, and, in that instant, out of nowhere came Stefan, his bright blue car charging hard on the inside. As I drifted up into the high groove of the banked corner, Tanaka snapped his car, low and to my left—and right into Stefan.

Chapter 18

Air Show

Three stock cars might have had enough room to make it through turn three, side by side, with some fender rubbing, but not three open-wheeled formula cars. At close quarters in a formula car, the worst case accident happens when you get your wheels interlocked with another car. It's a critical mistake that guarantees someone is going to get launched into the air—and Tanaka made it at 150 MPH. His left front wheel got into Stefan's right rear. When their two tires touched, the result was instant and terrifying. Out of the corner of my eye I saw the front of Tanaka's car vault into the air as Stefan spun out of control toward the grass infield.

I held my line in the high groove out of turn three and had an instant to check my mirrors before turning into four. What I saw was a split-second mental snapshot that I would never forget. Tanaka's car was completely inverted and on its way back to the hard asphalt upside down. Stefan's car was spinning across the infield grass. That was all I had time to take in as turn four rushed toward me. I banked the Swift into a low line and then on to the front straight. The yellow flags were already out and waving furiously as I passed the start-finish line. It had to be bad.

I was sure that Tanaka had come down squarely on his head, and I stopped myself from thinking about what the marshals were going to find back in turn three if he had. I caught up to a slowing DaSilva, lifted off myself, and tried to see something of what was going on behind me in my mirrors. It was useless. I had to wait until Raul and I came around to turn three again. The corner marshals were fast. They were already standing out on the track surface, slowing us right down to a crawl and directing traffic around the pieces of shattered black fiberglass. I told myself not to look, but I did. I had to know.

What remained of Tanaka's car had somehow come to rest right side up. It was little more than a ball of black wreckage. Its engine and gearbox had been torn off, as a single chunk of twisted metal, and were sitting fifty yards away from the shattered cockpit. All four wheels, both wings, and all of the bodywork were scattered in a field of debris that looked exactly like a plane crash—which, at the speeds we were doing, it had been. But the most incredible image was of Hiro Tanaka, alive, and in one piece, limping toward the ambulance with the help of a marshal. I immediately began looking for Stefan's bright blue number 7 car, but it was nowhere to be seen. That could only mean the tiny Frenchman had recovered from his spin and was back in the race somewhere behind me and Bennedetto.

All this happened on lap thirty-three, which brought out the Ferrari pace car again. As we all formed up in single file, I looked back over the field behind in my mirrors and saw with satisfaction that Stefan was there. He had survived, regained control of his car, and rejoined the pack in sixth place. It took ten laps under yellow before the wreckage was cleared. The pace car pulled off as we exited turn four. In that time, the tension really started to build. The field was tightly bunched in single file and, with the caution period delays, everyone left would have good tires. Everything was shaping up for a real fight over the final laps.

Allan was ready.

"Going green! Going green!"

This time I was too close to Raul to create a gap, so

I just tucked underneath his rear wing and waited for him to nail it. I planned to race him down into turn one and see who lifted first.

I knew it wasn't going to be me.

The starter waited until we were almost past his box before waving the green flag. Raul and I both buried our right feet at the same second. It should have been a neck-and-neck drag race down the front straight, but it wasn't. It wasn't even close.

DaSilva's yellow car just streaked away from me with an incredible surge of power, actually breaking its rear tires loose as it clawed for traction. For a moment I thought that my engine had died, but it was pulling clean and hard, even leaving Bennedetto behind. It was unbelievable. All of the cars in the Formula Atlantic Series used the same Cosworth engines. They were built and tested in the same shop, and no further modifications were allowed, to ensure that they were all made with close to the same power. That's why the racing in the series was so close. Properly maintained, the engines were bulletproof; while some might be a shade better than others, the sudden acceleration of DaSilva's car was incredible. It was performing like it had double the power of anybody else, which I knew was physically impossible. All the cars were inspected before every race to make sure that no one was running a trick engine. But somehow Raul had found raw power that left everyone behind in the space of a few seconds.

There was absolutely no way to stay with him. All I could do was watch Raul easily pull out five car lengths going into turn one, hold that gap through two, and then disappear into the distance. By the end of that lap and the next, his lead was almost half a mile, the length of the main straight.

Chapter 19

Too Fast

I was stunned. I'd driven a strong, smart tactical race and worked up from fourteenth to second. I'd kept enough in reserve for the final five laps, where I was sure I could hunt down Raul and challenge him for the win. My tires were in great shape, the car was handling beautifully, and I had been all set for one last charge. Without Tanaka as a blocker, Raul would have had to defend his lead all by himself. I'd seen him in that position before and knew that he tended to become nervous and erratic under pressure. I had been counting on it to give me an opening.

None of this carefully planned strategy mattered now. DaSilva just flat drove away from me and everyone else. I couldn't believe that he'd just been cruising around until these last few laps. Raul was quick, but I knew that he had never been that much faster than the rest of us. I pushed as hard as I could for the next three laps, using up everything that was left in my tires. But still Raul stretched his lead as the laps wound down.

Bennedetto had gradually dropped away from third place. But then I saw Stefan's blue car growing larger in my mirrors, fighting hard. We blasted past the pits together and I caught a glimpse of Herb's pit board:

P2
L48
- 20
32.3

It was my fastest lap of the race and I still couldn't catch Raul. I could see that the distance between us wasn't growing anymore, and he seemed to have eased up. But we both knew that I was in a distant second place, and there were only two laps left. Even though Stefan and I were running together as hard as we could, Raul had a 20-second cushion on us, and had the power to add to it if needed. Unless his car died, or he did something really stupid, I knew then that it was over. Raul DaSilva could not be caught.

Stefan and I went flat out over the last two laps, but we were really only racing each other for second place. My tires were finally gone, and it looked like

Stefan's were as well. We slid and weaved through the final corners and charged hard to the finish line side by side in a photo finish, the nose of his car just inches ahead of mine to take second place.

As we took the checkered flag and lifted off, Stefan looked over and gave me a thumbs-up from his cockpit. I waved back, but it was a gesture of friendship rather than celebration. We had driven hard, raced each other almost to a dead heat, and finished second and third. We were on the victory podium all right, but not in the top place. We both knew that our championship hopes were gone. DaSilva had just won the race, and with it, enough points to take the North American Formula Atlantic Championship—just like he said he would.

It was my third time standing on the podium in as many races. But I felt none of the satisfaction that had come with my second place at Milwaukee or my win in Toronto. Raul laughed, beamed, and gloated in his victory, while Stefan and I smiled thinly. We then stood stone-faced as the Brazilian national anthem was played in honor of the new series champion. Raul pulled on a baseball cap that read, Raul DaSilva Formula Atlantic Champion. All of his crew members did the same. They were so confident of victory that they'd had the championship caps made up before the race. DaSilva was beside himself with excitement, playing to the crowd, posing for the photographers, and showering himself with champagne.

Stefan and I accepted our trophies quietly and left our champagne corked.

I don't like to lose, but at the same time I certainly respect excellence in competition and don't mind shaking the hand of anyone who has earned it. But at that moment, I felt no respect for Raul and was in no mood to celebrate. Something wasn't right.

Behind us was a large video screen with the final top three in the series displayed for all to see:
North American Formula Atlantic Championship: Final Championship Standings

> Raul DaSilva, São Paulo, Brazil
>
> Stefan Veilleux, Bordeaux, France
>
> Eddie Stewart, Vancouver, Canada

Although we shook hands with Raul to congratulate him, neither Stefan nor I could get into the spirit of the moment. We were crushed that he had won by such a huge margin. He'd hammered us in front of thousands of spectators, a large TV audience, and our own team members. That was hard enough. But there was still something else bothering me that made this defeat even harder to swallow. It wasn't just disappointment due to defeat. I could have accepted that from Stefan, who had driven brilliantly.

But not from Raul DaSilva. It was how he'd done it. It was just too easy. I didn't think that he'd had to race hard to win, and I knew that he wasn't good enough to deserve it. And that started me thinking about why his bright yellow car was so much faster than ours—too fast.

Chapter 20

Protest

Stefan and I put on our plastic smiles. We posed for a few more pictures then stepped down from the podium. We left Raul to celebrate with his crew, his girlfriends, and his pack of millionaire friends. As we walked behind the stage, I stopped and took Stefan's aside.

"Stefan, wait a second. I'm not a sore loser but this just rips me."

He looked up at me with blank, tired eyes, and shrugged.

"He has done it, Eedie, no? We did not having the speed."

"Maybe," I said. "But in all the races you've driven—all summer in this series and last year in Europe—have you ever seen a car walk away from everyone like Raul did today?"

Stefan thought about it then shook his head. "*Non.*

Never I am seeing this."

"Exactly! And that's why I can't accept this. Look, Stefan. I had lunch with Raul yesterday. He offered me a place on his team. He even tried to bribe me but I turned him down. During that conversation he mentioned to me, twice, that he was sure he would have the best car in the race today. He was really confident about that. And a few weeks back, I talked with Kurt Heinrich before Raul fired him. He told me that Raul's crew was working on something new and secret— something to do with the fuel injection on the engine. So, what if DaSilva's guys did something to get more power, a lot more power, out of his engine?"

Stefan considered this for a few moments and then shook his head.

"*Non*. You cannot. All engine, they are the same. Sealed. Can't touch. Against the rule."

Stefan was right. The series rules clearly stated that Cosworth built the same engine in exactly the same way for everyone, and then they sealed the engine to prevent anyone changing parts or tampering with them. All you were allowed to do was install, tune, and maintain them. It was a good rule, which made sure everyone had reliable engines with equivalent power. It also prevented the big-money teams from building monster engines that only they could afford.

It kept things equal for everyone, which put the focus on driving and teamwork, rather than raw power and money. And on top of that, all the cars were inspected before each race; and all the top finishers were inspected after every race to make sure that no one had broken an engine seal or done anything illegal to their cars. The penalty for anyone who did was severe—instant disqualification from the race and the loss of any points earned for the season.

I knew that it would be almost impossible for anyone to tamper with an engine and get away with it. But there was also no doubt in my mind that if anyone was going to try it, Raul was the guy. It was the only explanation that could account for his car's massive power—and he was arrogant enough to think that he could get away with it. I studied Stefan as he came to the same conclusion.

"Eedie, this is a big thing you are saying. It is the illegal. If true, Raul is out."

"Yes, he is. Out of this race and out of the series. And you would be the champion, Stefan."

He nodded slowly.

"*Oui*. Yes, I know this. I think also, he was too fast. And Raul, he has to win. So he is the cheater guy, no?"

"No—I mean yes. He could have cheated. I'm convinced he did. His car will be weighed and get the general inspection along with ours. They'll check the engine seals, but that won't be enough to find out if something's up. There has to be an official protest, which will get the inspectors to look deeper. Specifically it has to protest the fuel-injection system of Raul's engine. That's the one place they need to look, and it has to be gone over with a microscope. If something's wrong it must be proven, and only a technical inspector can make that call. But listen, Stefan. It will not happen unless someone steps up and files an official protest against Raul in the next hour. I'm prepared to do that. Right now."

"And if you are wrong, Eedie?" Stefan asked.

"Then I'll be wrong. I'll lose the protest fee, I'll apologize, and I'll look like a jerk who doesn't know how to play fairly. I'll take that gamble. If I'm right, Stefan, he's busted. Raul will get what he really deserves and so will you. You'll take the championship you earned today. But if I do nothing, he wins all around. And I'll always wonder."

Stefan nervously ran his hands through his thick, curly hair and paced back and forth. Filing an official protest was a serious step—not the sort of action to be taken lightly. Basically, you were openly—publicly and in writing—accusing another driver of cheating. If you were wrong and his car was legal, then you would be seen by race fans, the media, and your fellow competitors as nothing but a whiner and a sore loser from that day forward. Stefan stopped pacing, placed his hands on his hips, and set his jaw.

"OK. I am getting this. It is not for you to doing this, Eedie. It is the thing for me, myself. I am the man of the race. If I am to losing the championship, it must be fair. So, the protests I am filing! Come, we go together."

Chapter 21

Two Things

We found the chief race steward in his office, where Stefan asked for the official forms. I helped him fill out the papers and write up the exact details of what might be illegal with DaSilva's engine. Then we went back to our separate pits to wait.

Allan and J.R. met me on the way back and congratulated me on finishing third. Then I filled them in on the protest.

We reached our pit and said goodbye to the wheelchair kids. Trevor was the last to get on the bus, but before he went up the ramp, he called me over.

"Hey, Eddie, thanks, man! This whole weekend was just excellent!" he exclaimed.

"All right, Trevor. Maybe we'll do it again sometime."

"Yeah! And that DaSilva guy? No way he outdrove you and Stefan, Eddie. No way!"

"Maybe you're right, Trevor. Watch the sports pages. There might be an interesting story there tomorrow."

"Hey, I know I'm right. Something's bogus on that car, guaranteed. See ya!" he yelled as he bounced his chair up the ramp and into the bus.

J.R. and Susan grinned broadly and waved good-bye. Then they called everyone into the garage and sat us all down. J.R. firmly closed the overhead door then waited for absolute silence. He stood with his hands on his hips and fire in his eyes as his gaze scanned each of our silent faces. J.R. looked every inch the NFL linebacker, and he wasn't smiling anymore.

"I want to say three things," he began, pacing the floor. "First, you should all know that Stefan Veilleux has filed a protest against Raul DaSilva. Eddie has passed on information to Stefan, and the officials are inspecting the car now. Their decision could very well change the outcome of this race and decide the championship. Eddie's stepped up with that information and acted on his conscience. Win or lose the protest, he's done the right thing. I want you to know that I fully respect that."

"As do we all," Allan stated, looking at me with approval.

"Agreed," J.R. continued. "Second, as the sponsor of this team I want all of you to know exactly how I feel right now. We gave Eddie a great car today and he drove it well. But he didn't win. The season is finished, over. And you know what? I'm proud of every one of you. We raced smart and hard, right down to the final lap, and got nosed out by maybe three inches. That's an effort to be proud of, ladies and gentlemen. And depending on what we hear about this protest, we may just finish runner-up in the series. There's no shame in that for a brand new team and a rookie driver. Today was a good day for us all. So don't you dare let me see anyone on my team moping around, hanging their head! Are we clear?"

We all sat wide-eyed and nodded silently as J.R.'s voice boomed off the concrete walls. We were clear. Crystal.

"All right, then," said J.R. as he sat down and winked at Susan.

Everyone was mentally counting to three.

"J.R.?" Rick asked meekly.

"Yes, Rick?"

"You, uh…you said that you had three things to say. You've still got one left."

J.R.'s smile returned. "I know. I'm saving that for later."

Chapter 22

Truth

I hate to wait. Always have. I'll drive across town to get around a traffic jam, or come back later rather than stand in line. So sitting in our garage, staring at the walls, and waiting for a decision on Stefan's protest was about as appealing as watching paint dry. After ten minutes of that, I decided to walk back to the victory podium stage with Herb, Allan, and J.R..

There was still a large crowd. Raul signed autographs and did interviews, telling everyone what a great race he'd run and how he was all set to move up to Champ Cars next year. Obviously he hadn't yet been told that his car and the race results had been protested. That changed as we joined the crowd around the podium.

It was all going perfectly for Raul until an official took him aside for a few quiet words. Raul's grin rapidly faded and was replaced by shock—and then something I hadn't seen from him before. I had expected his usual fit of violent rage, but this time DaSilva looked small and scared. He said nothing as he snapped his fingers at his crewmen and briskly led the Ascension Motorsports team off the stage and through the crowd.

The official stepped up to the microphone. "Ladies and gentlemen, it is my duty to inform you that the results of this race are suspended. A protest has been filed by Veilleux Racing against the winning car, number 4, entered by Ascension Motorsports and driven by Raul DaSilva. The car is being inspected now and we will announce the findings shortly. Until a decision on the protest is reached, there will be no official results announced for this race, or for the championship."

The crowd slowly broke up into murmuring groups. We talked for a few minutes with some of the fans and I did a quick interview with a magazine writer, who was sure I would be getting the Rookie of the Year Award. That would be nice, but I was far more interested in the protest. We decided to stop by Stefan's pit to see if he'd heard anything, but we found it strangely quiet with the overhead garage door closed.

I walked over to the small entrance door and peered

into the window. Raul and about a dozen Ascension Motorsports guys had backed Stefan and all six of his crew members into a corner of the shop. I couldn't hear what they were saying, but from the tense expressions on the faces of Stefan and his crewmen, I had a very good idea of the topic of conversation. DaSilva was demanding that Stefan withdraw his protest. Immediately. For his trouble Stefan could choose between a bag of money or a broken face. It would make no difference to Raul, as long as Stefan backed down.

I quickly motioned to the others to follow me as I opened the door and stepped into the garage. Everyone turned and watched the four of us walk in and close the door. The air was alive with tension, and our arrival cranked it up another notch. Raul turned and took a few steps toward us, sounding tough as nails—with twelve of his crewmen behind him.

"Get out, Stewart! There is nothing here that concerns you," he snapped.

"We're here to visit a friend," I replied evenly and then glanced at Stefan. "Unless of course this is a bad time. Want us to come back later, Stefan?"

"*Non!*" Stefan shouted. "Please for you are staying now, Eedie!"

I looked hard at DaSilva.

"Looks like we're welcome. If anyone needs to leave, Raul, I'm thinking maybe it's you and your guys. It's getting a little crowded in here."

Raul didn't blink. "I will tell you a final time, Stewart. Leave now—while you still can."

Before I could reply, J.R. and Herb stepped up beside me. At most, I'm about five foot eight and 150 pounds soaking wet, but those two were both well over six foot four and 250 pounds. And from their stances and expressions, there was no doubt in any-one's mind that they meant business.

"No. You wouldn't want to try that," Herb said evenly. "Here's what you *can* do, though, Raul. Eddie's going to go over and open the overhead door. And then you and your crew can walk out of here."

"No one tells me what I can do!" Raul snarled. "Or my men!"

J.R. walked slowly across the floor, past Raul, and stood right in front of the biggest guy in Raul's group. He stared him down and then ran his gaze slowly over the rest. Most of them were staring at their shoes.

"Your men? I wouldn't be counting too much on the guys behind you, Raul," he replied, shaking his head slowly. "No. They don't look like they're ready to defend the honor of their fearless leader. And they don't look stupid either."

J.R. stepped back, towering above Raul as he fixed him with a cold, hard stare.

"They know some things. They know you ordered them here to threaten Stefan. They know what you made them do to your car. And they know that you're about to get caught, disqualified from this race, and lose the championship and maybe even your team. They know now that it's all coming undone. You're going to lose, Raul, and you seem to be the only guy in the room who doesn't know it. That's why, when that door opens, they'll leave."

"Open it, Edward," Allan ordered.

I walked past Raul and his crewmen, silently hoping J.R. was right and that I wasn't about to be jumped from behind. I felt their eyes on my back as I unlocked the overhead door and rolled it up, opening the garage to the noise and bustle of the pit lane.

Nobody moved for a few seconds, and then, one by one, the crewmen of Ascension Motorsports quietly shuffled out of Stefan's garage until Raul stood alone. He turned to Stefan.

"Veilleux, if you do not withdraw this protest, I will—"

"You will do nothing," Allan snapped. "It's over, Raul, and it's not Stefan's fault or anyone else's. You did it to yourself."

Raul glared at us for a moment. Then he stormed out. There was absolutely nothing he could say.

The truth is like that.

Chapter 23

DaSilva's Reward

We watched DaSilva as he turned and left, walking at first before breaking into a run back to his motor home. We waited with Stefan and his crew in his motor home and drank coffee for two hours. Finally there was a knock on the door. A track marshal told us that the officials had completed their inspection of Raul's car. Stefan was required to attend a meeting to hear the decision.

A small room in the control tower had been hastily set up. It was jammed with reporters, officials, marshals, drivers, and crew members. Rick, Herb, and I stood at the back with Stefan, who was growing increasingly pale and nervous by the minute. There was no sign anywhere of Raul or any of his crew. The race steward went to a small podium and tapped the microphone, to make sure it was working, as the TV lights came on and the cameras rolled.

"Thank you, everyone, for your patience. As you are aware, a protest was filed after today's race by competitor Stefan Veilleux against the number 4 car owned by Ascension Motorsports and driven by Raul DaSilva. Mr. Veilleux alleged in his protest that the fuel-injection system of Mr. DaSilva's car did not meet series regulations. Our head technical inspector, Ken Shields, with the aid of factory engineers from Cosworth, has examined Mr. DaSilva's car. I will now ask him to present his findings. Mr. Shields."

A tall, middle-aged man with thick, wire-rimmed glasses and a gray ponytail stepped up to the microphone and read from a clipboard.

"The first three cars, including car number 4, were inspected for weight, track, wheelbase, aerodynamics, and engine seals. All cars passed inspection in these areas. Car 4 was then further inspected to determine if its fuel-injection system met series regulations."

He paused and looked over his glasses at the packed, silent room.

"We found nothing wrong with the fuel-injection system of car number 4."

The silence was immediately shattered by dozens of raised voices, some supportive, some questioning—

most of them surprised. Stefan shaded his eyes in humiliation. He knew that when this was over, he, not Raul, would be the outcast. I searched again for Raul, without success.

"However..." With that single word, Tech Inspector Shields instantly silenced the room.

"In our inspection, we *did* find something irregular on car 4 related to fuel. As you may know, all cars in this series must use gasoline from the series supplier. Nothing may be added to it. As the results of today's race will decide the North American Formula Atlantic Championship, we included fuel-system testing in the inspection. All of the top three cars were tested. I regret to inform you that one of them was found to be illegal."

That got everyone buzzing again. I nudged Stefan.

"Stefan!" I hissed in his ear. "I know we used series gas. What about you? Put some of your dad's stuff in your tank?"

"Eedie, do not make the joke! Veilleux wines are too good for the racing cars."

Mr. Shields then held up a red metal cylinder, about the size of a large bottle of fruit juice.

"Some of you will recognize this as a fire-extin-guisher bottle. It is a required safety item on all Atlantic series cars, and it is bolted under the driver's seat. In the event of a fire, the driver can press a button and discharge the contents of this bottle to put out a fire inside the cockpit. Our inspection, however, revealed that this bottle did not contain the normal fire-extinguisher material. We discovered that it was instead filled with nitrous oxide gas, which was released into the fuel-injection system by a small switch that we found behind the accelerator pedal."

The crowd buzzed again.

There were enough people with drag racing knowledge in the room who knew what nitrous oxide (or NOX) could do. One of them was a burly guy behind me, who explained to everyone within earshot that when NOX was mixed with gasoline, you got an instant explosion of massive power—sometimes almost double what you normally would have. That meant that, with a shot of NOX, a standard 300-horsepower Cosworth Atlantic engine suddenly became a 500-horsepower rocket. You couldn't use it for long without melting the engine, but the bottle Mr. Shields was showing held enough NOX for a few well-timed shots, which a driver could call up when he needed to blast away into the distance—exactly like Raul DaSilva had done to me in those final few laps.

The race steward replaced Tech Inspector Shields at the microphone.

"Thank you, Mr. Shields. My thanks also to Sarturo Nakajima and Don Williams from Cosworth. Based upon the findings of the technical inspection of Ascension Motorsports car number 4, I hereby make the following ruling. The protest filed by Mr. Veilleux is upheld. Car number 4 is disqualified from the results of today's race. Any points earned today by Mr. DaSilva are rescinded, and all points awarded to Mr. DaSilva over the course of this season are hereby forfeited. I will also be making a recommendation in my report that Mr. DaSilva's competition license be suspended for a period of one year."

The room was dead still again, but this time it wasn't in anticipation of the verdict—it had been announced, and it was major. Raul and his team had been caught cheating. They had been punted from the race, from the entire championship, and Raul was going to lose his license as well. The race steward let everyone take it all in for a few moments before he took a deep breath, put the clipboard aside, and relaxed with a warm smile.

"And now on to more pleasant business. I can officially announce the revised results for today's race. First place and double-points are awarded to Veilleux Racing car number 7, driven by Stefan Veilleux. Second place is awarded to car number 28, DynaSport

Motorsports, driven by Eddie Stewart. Third place is awarded to Team Milano car number 50, driven by Elio Bennedetto. The rest of the final positions will be posted after this meeting."

There was a wave of strong applause from the crowd in recognition of the three top finishers and also for the thorough job that the officials had done in exposing DaSilva. I'd already added up the championship points in my head and knew exactly what was coming next.

"Finally, these results allow me to announce, with pleasure, that the North America Formula Atlantic Championship is hereby awarded to Stefan Veilleux! Where are you, Stefan?"

The room exploded in cheers and applause and everyone was turning to see where Stefan was in the crowd. At five foot five, he was hard to spot, but I knew where to look.

He was on the floor.

Stefan had passed out in shock the moment that the race steward announced the title win. He had crumpled against Herb and slid into a ball at our feet. We picked him up under his arms, Rick grabbed his feet, and we carried him out of the cramped meeting room. His victory speech would have to wait.

Chapter 24

The Third Thing

S tefan pushed his toes deep into the warm Florida sand, stretched in his canvas beach chair, and scratched Clarence behind the ears. A few days back at the Reynolds' beach house outside Miami had resulted in a full recovery. Stefan was finally able to appreciate the fact that he was a champion. The large silver trophy that proved it was parked next to his chair, and Stefan carried it everywhere as a reminder that he had really won the title.

John and Susan Reynolds hosted a party at their beach house. It ran for three days. As well as our team, Stefan's crew was invited, along with Elio Bennedetto's entire team. Sophie and Elio spoke and laughed together in rapid Italian, and the kitchen and dining room became a small restaurant as Sophie cooked for thirty again. Clarence did nonstop house tours for all the guests, and Caroline ran video high-lights of the season on the huge plasma TV in the theater room. The rest of us did some waterskiing and swimming, and Elio and his crew crushed everyone at beach volleyball. But mostly we just relaxed in the sun and put things in order.

It had been an excellent season for all of us—Stefan's first major title, top-three finishes for Elio, and the Rookie of the Year Award for me. Even better, there had been no sign at all of Raul DaSilva, who apparently had left the country as fast as he could.

A few short months ago, I would have been satisfied with just making some west coast pro races in our home-built Mustang. I had a lot to be thankful for, and I made time to say so personally to everyone over the next three days.

On the last morning, as we packed up to leave, I had something special to say to Caroline, but, as ever, she was a step ahead of me. I got the details during a final long walk on the beach.

"Eddie, I'm taking Sophie on a holiday. We're leaving this afternoon for two months in Greece and Italy. Kind of an art and restaurant tour," she said.

"You guys planning to do any cliff diving in the Greek Islands?"

"No! I'm keeping her out of the water. She's got lots

of family in Italy and I am, after all, her official driver. So we'll just take it slow, day by day—and no swimming demonstrations. So…you'll miss me?" she stated with a smile.

"Yes, I will. And what happens when you get back?" I asked.

"Well, you've got some decisions to make. But before you do, I think you'll want to hear what J.R. has to say at lunch."

Our farewell lunch was served on the huge rear deck and featured a truly international assortment of pancakes, waffles, French crepes for Stefan, fresh fruit,

and special syrup blends—all expertly prepared by Herb. Some things never change.

At the end of the meal, J.R. stood, raised his mug of real coffee, and proposed a toast.

"To this shattering coffee, to friendship, and to excellence. May they all long continue."

Everyone clinked whatever they were drinking

and gave their full attention to our host.

"Before all of you leave today, Susan and I want you to know how much we've enjoyed this season and getting to know all of you. And we have a little something for our new champion."

Stefan rose and stood sheepishly beside J.R. as Susan handed him a plain brown paper bag. Stefan opened it and pulled out a bright red T-shirt with a simple message in gold letters: Fast Eddie Stewart is My Hero!

We clapped and whistled as Stefan grinned broadly, pulled it on and held up his hand for quiet.

"Thank you. Merci, J.R. and Susan. You are fantastics. All of you are the best and the friends to me. And this shirt is to mean as much for you as to win the championship had meant to me also. So now, what will you do? Caroline and Sophie, they are to Greece for to have the holiday. Allan, he is to England. Eedie, Herb, and Rick, they are to Seattle. And Elio he is already gone home to Italy from yesterday. So, I am to think to myself. 'Stefan,' I say, 'should this be the end?'"

I glanced over at Caroline and Rick, but they just shrugged. Whatever Stefan had up his sleeve, it was a mystery to us.

"So," he continued. "My father Jacques and me, we

have the talks last night. He is very happy for me. And he is also a man of the race. Then I talk with J.R. We talk a very long time. And there is a plan."

J.R. stood and took over from Stefan, who returned to his deck chair, placed his trophy firmly in his lap, looked over at me, and grinned.

"Last week I told my team that I had three things to say to them. As Rick reminded me, I only said two. Well, now it's time for the third thing. Susan and I have had such a great time with this that we have decided a few things. DynaSport Industries is going to stay in racing, and this is going to be our team. What we have in mind is this."

He held up a copy of a racing magazine with a picture of the opening lap of the Le Mans 24-hour race on the cover.

"For me, there are three major races in the world, the triple crown of motorsport—the Indy 500, the Daytona 500, and the 24 Hours of Le Mans in France. Some day, I'd like to see one of our cars in each of them. We're not ready for something like Indy or Daytona yet. But Stefan, his father, and I all think that, between our two teams, we have the core of a new team that could take a serious run at Le Mans next year—in our own cars and with Eddie and Stefan as lead drivers. How about it?"

I took maybe a second to decide that I was in, and I got instant nods of approval from Rick, Herb, and Allan. I suspected that Sophie and Caroline already knew, as they were grinning at us. Stefan's crew chattered excitedly to each other in rapid French.

J.R. was right. Le Mans was possible. It was flat-out day and night racing, with 200 MPH blasts down the Mulsanne straight, in the French countryside. The 24 Hours of Le Mans was a world-class event—the ultimate test of endurance for a race car, a team, and its drivers.

And next summer, were going to make some thunder roll on Mulsanne.

Caution period. A point when the race is slowed to allow the track to be cleared.

Champ Car. A formula race car competing in the Champ Car World Series.

Data acquisition. A computer system that collects information on race car performance.

Downforce. The load placed on a car by airflow over its front and rear WINGS.

Formula Atlantic. A single seat, open-wheeled race car.

Gearbox. Contains gears that the driver shifts to transmit engine power to the wheels.

Grid. The starting lineup of cars, which is based upon qualifying times.

Marshals. Racetrack safety workers.

Oversteer. When the rear wheels lose their grip and a race car slides or spins.

Pace lap. A slow warm-up lap before starting the race.

Pace car. The official car that leads the race car field during the pace lap or caution period.

Pit. The area where teams work on the race cars.

Pit board. A sign that is held up by the pit crew to inform their driver of place, race position, and lap.

Push. Another term for UNDERSTEER.

Podium. A stage where the top three race finishers receive their awards.

Pole position. The first starting position, which is awarded to the fastest qualifier.

Qualifying. Timed laps that determine where each car will be positioned at the start of the race.

Setup. Adjustments that are made to the race car by crew members.

Suspension. A system of springs, shocks, and levers that are attached to the wheels and support the race car.

Trans-Am. The Trans-American Championship for modified sports cars.

Understeer. When the front wheels lose their grip and the race car continues straight rather than turning.

Wings. Direct airflow that passes over the race car, pushing it down onto the track.

ANTHONY HAMPSHIRE is as comfortable strapped into the seat of a race car as he is in front of a classroom. Raised in London, England, and Calgary, Alberta, Anthony has been a racing driver and team manager, a football coach, and a magazine columnist. He was also a classroom teacher and educational technology consultant and is now a school principal. Anthony has earned national and provincial awards for his work in school curriculum and media, authored educational software, and is a regular conference presenter and workshop leader. He makes his home at the foot of the Rocky Mountains in Alberta, where he lives with his wife, two daughters, and a bossy Welsh Corgi.